MW01165479

Perfect

Published by Ventana Publishing, LLC

KimberlyKeagan.com

Paperback ISBN: 979-8-9925731-0-7

A captivating story of love transcending social divides and family sacrifice, set during New York's Gilded Age. William and Ivy's journey—from rivals to kindred spirits —is a testament to courage, faith, and the power of love. A must-read for historical romance fans!

— N.Y. DUNLAP, AUTHOR OF *THE MISADVENTURES OF ITCHY IZZY*

Perfect is an endearing story of two imperfect people who find out that despite their unique flaws and class differences, they are matched perfectly. Kimberly Keagan does a beautiful job of weaving Gilded Age history into this timeless romantic journey that makes their happily ever after as vibrant and real as if it happened yesterday.

— SOPHIE LEIGH FOX, AUTHOR OF *THE DUKE'S LAST WORD*

Keagan's beautifully written historical stays with you long after the last page is read. Two souls sensing their own flaws, both from different worlds, as they navigate the trials set before them, and find their perfection and acceptance in the eyes of the other.

— CHRISTINA RICH, AUTHOR OF *A HUSBAND FOR AN AMISH BRIDE*

Kimberly Keagan's debut novel is *Perfect*. And not just the title. The setting of Manhattan, New York in 1895, and the rise of the department store, was a wonderful backdrop for this historical inspirational romance. Will and Ivy grabbed my heart from the very beginning. Kimberly weaves a beautiful story of two people whose different worlds intertwine in ways that weren't quite clear at first, yet ultimately turned into something perfect in every way. I can't wait to read more from this author.

— DENISE M. COLBY, AUTHOR OF *WHEN PLANS GO AWRY*

Kimberly Keagan's stories immerse you in the historical era with rich detail, lovely settings, and characters you want to spend time with. This delightful novel about a shopgirl and a rich department store heir (perhaps the precursor of *You've Got Mail)* shows the power of love to overcome life's challenges.

— MAIRE WELLS COUTU, AWARD-WINNING AUTHOR AND SPEAKER

PERFECT

HEARTS ON DISPLAY

BOOK ONE

KIMBERLY KEAGAN

For my husband, who is perfect for me.

ONE

Friday, May 24, 1895
Blackwing Hall, Pennsylvania

The drawing room clock chimed midnight.

William Walraven searched the faces of Blackwing Hall's elegant guests as they ascended the grand staircase to the second floor. He slid a hand into his jacket pocket, double-checking that the velvet jeweler's box was still safely tucked away, and weaved his way through the crowd.

A small orchestra entertained the gathering from behind artfully arranged palms and ferns in the ballroom. Will spotted his mother and made his way in her direction. As he passed a group of women, the gloved hand of a well-respected society matron grasped his forearm in a surprisingly firm hold. "I understand you're to announce your engagement tonight."

His eyes darted to his mother, who was obviously incapable of keeping a secret.

"Elizabeth Blake is perfect for you," the matron continued. "Your father is pleased, I'm sure, that your two families will have such an intimate connection." The yellow feather perched on the top of her head listed when she tipped her chin. "Where *are* the Blakes, by the way?"

"They'll be here shortly." Will gently extricated his arm from her grip. "It's wonderful to see you, but if you'll excuse me, I must join my family." What he really needed to do was find his missing bride-to-be.

Elizabeth's statuesque figure and golden-blonde tresses should make her easy to spot in the gathering of Philadelphia's high society. He crossed the chevron parquet floor, and when he'd reached his mother's side, he leaned in with a false air of nonchalance. "Where are the Blakes?" he asked in a hushed tone.

His mother, her chestnut hair artfully swept back with diamond-studded combs, whispered, "I have no idea. The Blakes are famous for their tardiness, but this is bordering on rude."

"I'm going to check outside to see if their carriage has arrived."

He skirted the edge of the room and exited through a pair of French doors that opened directly onto the terrace. A gentle night breeze carried the fragrance of grass and clean air, a welcome respite from the heavy scent of perfume and cigars inside the ballroom. He descended the granite steps to the garden path.

He'd looked forward to this event with great anticipation. His father planned to announce his retirement, and Will fully expected to take over as head of Denwall. With Elizabeth at his side, they'd make a powerful couple. A perfect pairing. He couldn't say they loved each other but assumed that would come with time. The important thing was that their formidable fathers approved.

Will stalked down the tree-lined driveway, his footsteps crunching on gravel as he searched in vain for any sign of the Blakes' carriage. The pale moon cast enough light to see, but the only movement came from tree branches swaying in the evening breeze.

Blast it all—where were they? Annoyance surfaced, quickly swallowed by concern. The road from Philadelphia wasn't always safe at night. Perhaps he should send his parents' coachman to look for them.

No. Elizabeth's father was notorious for his tardiness. The man would probably saunter in two hours late, full of elaborate excuses. With a frustrated sigh, Will turned back to the house, an imposing silhouette with its multi-faceted roofline rising majestically against the moonlit sky.

He returned to the party by way of the front door, heels tapping on the spacious hall's black and white marble floor. Taking the stairs two at a time, he moved quickly, and then wound through the guests to whom his family had promised several announcements.

Father, an imposing figure in black and white evening clothes, stood before the enormous Carrara-marble fireplace at the ballroom's north end. Close by, Denwall's co-founder and chief operating officer, James Dennison, clinked a silver spoon against his crystal glass.

"Can I have your attention, please?" Father's onyx eyes surveyed the room. "First, thank you all for coming tonight."

Will found his mother and two brothers clustered to the side of the room and squeezed in next to Bert. Ned, the youngest of the three brothers, stood on the opposite side of their mother.

Once the room quieted, Father continued his rehearsed speech. "As you all know, James and I opened the first Denwall department store almost thirty years ago. Thanks to hard work and the patronage of the Philadelphia community, we've made a good go of it."

The guests tittered at the quip.

"Tonight, however, I'm announcing my retirement. I look forward to improving my golf game, but more importantly, to spending more time with my lovely wife."

The guests lifted their glasses in unison. "Hear, hear," some called out.

What Philadelphia society didn't know was that Father had a

weak heart, and the doctor had strongly advised him to retire. Otherwise, the head of Denwall would never consider stepping down. Charles Walraven didn't think anyone could run the company as well as he, not even his partner, James Dennison.

"Thank you. Enjoy the rest of your evening." Father threw back the last of his champagne and moved toward Mother's side. He gave her a tender kiss on the cheek, and she pulled him into an embrace. Mother was devoted to Father and well-suited to be the wife of a prominent businessman. Will wanted their kind of marriage for himself.

Father's demeanor hardened, however, when he looked at his two older sons. "I'd like to speak to you." He tipped his head toward Will and Bert. "Let's go out on the patio."

They passed through the French doors and strode across the terrace, away from the din of the ballroom. The Walraven patriarch had hinted at a family announcement several times over the past week.

Will's nerves jittered. Finally, his prayers would be answered, and he'd take his place at the helm of Denwall.

"I wanted you two to hear the news first," Father said when they'd reached the terrace railing.

Arms at his sides, Will prepared to shake his father's hand. Maybe they'd even embrace. Or maybe not. Father wasn't affectionate with his sons.

"I've asked one of our board members to step in and help James until we decide on a chief executive officer." Father's deep voice didn't waver, and he didn't look away.

Will shot Bert a look, and his stomach clenched. He should have known his father still didn't trust him, nor did he believe his second-born son worthy of running his precious business. "What do you mean by *until we decide*?"

Father put a palm out to stop further interruption. "Let me finish. James and I have long considered an expansion into the New York market, so it should come as no surprise that we're entering negotiations for a building and expect to sign documents in the next few weeks."

Will didn't like the direction of this conversation. Not one bit.

"I want you two to manage the new enterprise. We're opening the store in early November to take advantage of the holiday season, and you two need to make sure everything goes smoothly. I'll also be keeping an eye on everything from here."

Bert shuffled his feet but, true to his quiet manner, said nothing.

Will's head began to pound. "You want us in New York? Now? I just bought a house, and I'm asking Elizabeth's father for her hand tonight. Everything's planned. She'll want me in Philadelphia during our engagement, not a hundred miles away."

Father narrowed his eyes. "Consider this a trial of sorts. Don't mess it up."

So, that's what this was all about. Father wanted to test Will and his loyalty to Denwall, intentionally pitting him against Bert to see if he would fail.

Will slumped against the railing.

A patio door opened, and Mother stepped out. "Charles, you've received a message from the Blakes." She handed her husband a white notecard.

Father unfolded the missive and turned it toward the lamplight. He said a few choice words and crumpled the note in his fist. His brows came together, and he poked a finger into Will's chest. "Did you do something to ruin your relationship with Elizabeth?"

Will's mind reeled, but he refused to take a step back. He was used to his father's high-handedness. "I don't know what you're talking about." His voice came out rough, like sandpaper.

"Mrs. Blake and her daughter are on their way to England," Father spat.

"What? No, it must be a mistake." Elizabeth hadn't said a word to Will about leaving the country. She was supposed to be here tonight.

Mother rested a hand on Father's arm and nudged him away from Will. "Does the note say anything else, Charles?"

Father took a deep breath and placed his hand over hers. As it always had, Mother's presence calmed the man's temper. "Apparently, Elizabeth's become engaged to Lord Cumbria."

Mother's eyes grew as wide as saucers. "Who's Lord Cumbria?"

"A British peer of the realm."

And like a candle's flame extinguished in one short breath, Will's plans turned to smoke. No perfect wife. No perfect life.

Two

Monday, August 12, 1895
Manhattan, New York

"We come together, ladies and gentlemen, to face a common enemy," a barrel-chested man with an enormous mustache shouted atop an overturned milk crate.

Ivy King stood at the edge of a growing crowd while men and women with wooden signs marched along the sidewalk. The midday summer heat caused rivulets of perspiration to trail down her back, and she switched her shopping basket to the other arm.

The tension in the air wound tight as a coiled spring. At least fifty men and women had gathered to listen, riveted to the engaging speaker. Ivy hadn't planned to stop. Still, she had no choice, seeing as she couldn't get around the congregation of increasingly agitated people. And she couldn't very well step into the busy street where she'd risk getting run over by a carriage, wagon, or cable car barreling through the Union Square District.

"We have allowed this enemy to make disastrous inroads, and the institution is now encroaching on our interests with the ultimate intent of obliterating us altogether." The speaker paused for effect, his gaze sweeping over the crowd. "I speak, my friends, of the department store." The words were overblown, and the rhetoric wasn't new. Nevertheless, heads bobbed in agreement. "Shop owners, let me ask you a question. What will we do about it? Shall we sit quietly in our places of business and supinely permit ourselves to be crushed to death, or shall we rise as one body and stand for our rights, as Americans should?"

Ivy huffed, unsure how small shop owners could unite to defeat the behemoth emporiums. Battle had waged against the department stores for several years, but the casualties mounted. Sadly, smaller shop owners couldn't compete against the big stores with capital and clout, and some businesses were forced to close their doors.

An enthusiastic protestor brushed by Ivy with a sign that read "Booksellers, Newsdealers, and Stationers Unite!" Ivy recognized the woman as the wife of one of her father's old friends, a fellow bookseller feeling the squeeze of increasing competition.

Concerned about the time, Ivy glanced at the watch hanging from her chatelaine. She'd promised her grandmother she'd be back in twenty minutes, just long enough to buy the rolls for their lunch and a canister of coffee. If she tarried too long, Gran would worry.

Someone jostled her basket. "Pardon me," he said.

The deep but pleasant voice made Ivy lift her face. She found warm hazel eyes framed in long, dark eyelashes gazing back.

Oh, my. What a handsome man!

Having lived in the neighborhood her entire life, she knew most people from the area. This man, with a charming cleft chin, didn't look familiar. His hair appeared brown in the shadow of the buildings, but it would probably take on an altogether different hue in full sunlight. Chestnut, maybe. His expensive suit, tailored to perfection, emphasized his broad shoulders, and something about his confident yet kind bearing made her pulse quicken.

No matter. Ivy had no time to listen to verbose speeches or admire handsome men. Turning, she collided with a protestor's wooden sign. She stepped to the side but was closer to the curb than she realized. A sharp pain shot up her left leg as her ankle buckled, and she started to fall into the street. Her hands flew out to stop her face from smashing into the Belgian block that rushed to greet her. An arm grabbed her around the waist and pulled her back onto the sidewalk just as a beer wagon barreled by.

When her knight in shining armor gently set her down, Ivy gasped at the searing pain in her ankle. Slowly, she turned and lifted her chin to find the face of her rescuer. He was the man with the hazel eyes, and his arms held her upright, thank goodness. Otherwise, she would surely land in a heap at his feet.

"Are you all right?"

"Yes, thanks to you." Ivy tried to gather her wits. That was a narrow escape, and had he not grabbed her, she would have met her Maker that day. But to prove she was indeed fine, she took a tentative step.

Ouch, that hurt.

"I think I must have twisted my ankle when I fell." She clenched her teeth through the pain. Her ankle was on fire and if the stench emanating from her was any indication, she'd stepped into horse manure.

Wonderful. Could this day get any worse?

A policeman jostled by and his whistle pierced the air. "All right, folks, let's move along. You're blocking the sidewalk." People grumbled, but soon the crowd dispersed.

Ivy's rescuer put a firm hand under her elbow. "Can you walk?" he asked.

She drew in a breath, took another step, and grimaced. It was obvious she couldn't put weight on her left foot, which wasn't good, considering she already had a bad right leg. She glanced up to find his tall frame bent and his face close to hers.

"Are you with someone? Your husband, perhaps? I can find him for you."

Husband? Ivy almost snorted. Before that dream had become reality, her intended had run off with her best friend. "No, no. I'm not married. There's no husband." She babbled as his handsome countenance turned her brain to mush. Being this close to him, she could see tiny flecks of gold in his eyes.

"All right. Well, I'm William. Where were you headed, Miss...?"

"King." She tipped her head toward home. "I work at the bookshop on the corner, two blocks up."

"It's not far, but you can't get there on that ankle. You really should get a cab."

A cab fare for such a short ride—what a waste of money. The wealthy could be so frivolous. Ivy shook her head. "That's not necessary. I'll just walk slowly." She mentally smacked her forehead. He must think her a nincompoop.

With a hand on her forearm, he stopped her before she fell again and made a bigger fool of herself. "I'm paying for a cab to take you to work. I insist." He moved to her right side and held out his elbow. "Here. Take my arm and lean your weight on me as much as possible." They moved slowly but in tandem to the curb, and he raised his hand. A horse and carriage nosed its way over and pulled up next to them.

"Can I drive you somewhere, sir?"

William reached over and handed the cabbie some money. "Please take the lady to the bookshop two blocks up." He looked down at Ivy with raised eyebrows, and she nodded. "And when you arrive, ensure she gets to the door safely."

"Will do, sir." The driver looked at the bills in his hand. A grin split his face, and he tipped his hat. "Much obliged."

William took Ivy's hand, and she caught the pleasant scent of bay rum as he helped her into the carriage. His fingers were warm and strong around hers, and the brief contact sent tingles up her arm. Once she managed to get seated, he handed her the shopping basket she'd been carrying. "I think you dropped this. I'm afraid one of your rolls landed in the street."

Heat crept up Ivy's neck and infused her face as she took the basket from his hand. "Thank you, sir, for your kindness."

Closing the door, he stepped back and gave her a charming grin, causing her stomach to perform a circus act. "You're most welcome, Miss King." The carriage jolted and moved forward into traffic. Ivy turned and peered out the rear window. William was still at the curb, staring after her.

The carriage arrived at the bookshop shortly, and the driver jumped from his perch. After he opened her door, he held out his hand and helped Ivy alight. Following orders to take care of his passenger, he cupped her elbow and escorted her to the book-shop's front stoop. With a shoulder, he pushed open the front door.

Dickens, their Saint Bernard, met Ivy at the front door, tail wagging. Gran sat behind the counter, her nose in a book. She looked up, eyes wide behind her spectacles.

"What on earth?" Gran dropped the book and rushed over. Even at seventy, she was still spry. "Ivy, what's happened? Are you all right, dear?" Her aged brow furrowed. "Are you overheated?" She touched her granddaughter's forehead, but Ivy gently pressed her hand away.

"No, I'm not hot, Gran. Just twisted my ankle on the way back from the baker's. A kind gentleman ordered a cab to bring me back." Ivy hobbled to the counter.

"You should have a doctor take a look at you."

Good advice, certainly, but they couldn't afford a doctor right now. "I'll be fine."

"Weren't watching where you were walking, I suspect." Gran straightened and pursed her lips. Ivy almost snorted at the lecture from a woman who often read and walked simultaneously.

"Do you work here, miss?" the driver, who hovered nearby, asked.

Ivy leaned her weight on the counter. "My late father, Richard King, owned the shop. Now, my grandmother and I run it."

Fortunately, he didn't comment that she needed a husband to help her—like so many did when they realized she was unmarried—or else she might have lost her last shred of dignity and cried like a baby.

He turned toward the door. "Well, good day to you both."

"Thank you so much for your assistance." Gran gave him a warm smile. Once he'd crossed the threshold, she guided Ivy to one of the two reading chairs by the window. "Who was the gentleman who paid that driver?"

Ivy took slow, tentative steps and eased her behind into the seat. "I have no idea."

In a city the size of New York, with thousands of men named William, she doubted she'd ever see him again.

More's the pity.

—————

With long, quick strides, Will made his way down Fourteenth Street. His heart thudded in his chest, not from the brisk walk, but because saving someone from falling in front of an oncoming beer wagon did that to a man.

Thank you, Lord, for placing me at the right place at the right time.

Truth be told, he'd given Miss King several sideways glances while stuck in a logjam of people on the sidewalk. When his arm grazed hers, and she peered up at him, the breath had whooshed from his lungs. A beauty with ink-black hair that curled slightly around a heart-shaped face, she possessed the bluest eyes he'd ever seen.

He noted her clothes were clean and pressed but not of the latest style. Yet she carried herself with a natural grace that the simple cut of her gown couldn't hide.

When she'd suddenly slipped, he'd been momentarily shocked but quickly pulled her up and back against him. The scent of honeysuckle had drifted up from her hair, and he forgot they were on a crowded street for a moment. Her small form fit perfectly in his arms.

He'd been surprised when she told him she wasn't married. Will prayed she wasn't fated to a life of back-breaking work like so many young, unmarried women in the city.

Glancing at his watch, he shouldered open the door of the newest addition to his family's real estate portfolio. Slats of wood covered broken windows, and shelves dangled from the walls or lay busted on the floor of the old dry goods store. Stale, dusty air tickled his nose, and he sneezed.

"Ah, there you are," James Dennison called from across the room. "Right on time, as usual." He took Will's outstretched hand in a firm grip. "Where's your brother?"

Good question. "Bert's been taking a walk to Madison Square Park every morning. Takes a book with him and sometimes loses track of time. But he should be here soon."

Bert wasn't trying to be rude, he just valued punctuality less than others. In his defense, he was never more than ten minutes late. Still, his habitual tardiness was a major point of contention with their father.

On the other hand, Father's partner never seemed to let it bother him.

"How was your trip?" Will asked.

"Fine, fine," James replied. "The train ride from Philadelphia allows me to catch up on reading."

"Everyone all right at home?"

"Yes, everyone's splendid. Myra's in a tizzy with news of all the Americans marrying British nobles. Thinks one, if not all of our girls, should be able to find a suitable husband amongst the peers of the realm."

Like many wealthy American mothers did.

Three months had passed since Will's fiancée left Philadelphia for England to marry—and subsidize—one such noble. After receiving the news by messenger the night of their engagement party, gossip spread through Philadelphia society like wildfire.

The desertion still bruised his pride.

James cleared his throat. "Sorry, Will. I wasn't thinking."

"Don't worry about it. I'm over Elizabeth."

"Good, good. She was all wrong for you, anyway."

Now he tells me.

"Change of subject, eh?" James clapped a hand on Will's shoulder. "Sounds like the final negotiations went well."

Will wholeheartedly agreed. "We got a fair deal. Secured the building, the store's remaining merchandise, and the stable and outfit, including delivery wagons and horses." With the money transferred to Heinrich, the former owner, the building was officially Denwall's as of the day before. An army of workers was expected on Monday to begin reconstruction and renovation. Despite not wanting to take on this job in the beginning, the prospect of moving forward sent a thrill of excitement through Will.

"Since I've been out of the country this past month, why don't you give me a rundown of your ideas for the place?" James waved a hand toward the stairs.

"Certainly." Since James was a much easier man to please than his father, Will was more than happy to show him around. "As you know, the building is eight stories—six floors above ground and a basement and subbasement below."

James walked beside Will in that easy-going stride of his.

"Besides ripping out much of the interior, the first order of business is to add more windows and, depending on the condition, replace existing ones." Will pointed to the storefront off Fifth

Avenue. "Next, all new shelves and display cases will be added. A pulley system will bring merchandise up from the delivery room in the subbasement to each floor."

James studied the room, and Will hoped his mentor could see past the debris to imagine the gem beneath. "What are your plans for the departments?"

"It will be much like our existing stores. The basement is devoted to furniture and carpets. The main and largest floor is women's clothing, primarily ready-to-wear, but there's also a fabric department. We've planned a rotunda, which can be viewed from the balconies of each floor above, so it needs to be spectacular—silks, velvets, laces, ribbons, gloves, handkerchiefs. You get the idea."

When James nodded, Will pointed upward. "On the second floor will be men's and children's clothing. The third is specialty dressmaking and millinery. There will be sectioned-off workrooms for the dressmakers. Home goods on the fourth. The fifth floor..." Will glanced at James and grinned. "This is Bert's favorite part, and it's nothing like we've ever done. The fifth floor will be devoted to stationery and reading material—books, magazines, and newspapers. We plan to specialize in engraving and heraldic work. Also, a small café will serve beverages, sandwiches, and pastries. And we'll reserve the sixth floor for offices and invoice rooms."

"What about toilets? I can't stand it when a store lacks sufficient customer facilities."

What was it with men over fifty and their obsession with lavatories? "Every floor possesses a full water supply, lavatories, and so on. Every part of the building is easily accessible by spacious stairways and the elevator. Don't worry, the customer's comfort is of utmost importance."

James let out a low whistle. "You've thought of everything. Can't imagine why people will want or need to go anywhere else, save grocery shopping."

"That's the idea." He had considered providing for as many

customer needs as possible, even ones the other Denwall stores had yet to supply.

James clapped a hand on Will's shoulder. "You're doing a marvelous job. As always."

"Thank you, sir. That means a lot coming from you." Will wished his father was as sure of his abilities.

As if reading his thoughts, James's hand squeezed in reassurance. "I know Charles can be a hard man. But he's very proud of you. He just has difficulty letting go."

"That's like saying Vanderbilt has a few dollars," Will muttered, and James chuckled.

"I'm going to look around some more. Come find me when Bert gets here."

Once James had wandered off, Will walked to the grimy windows bracketing the entry. Upon further inspection, all would need to be replaced. One more thing in a long list before the grand opening in November. Now, more than ever, Will needed to prove he was the best man to take his father's place alongside James. Although Father wanted to encourage competition between his older sons, he obviously didn't know Bert very well. Or chose to ignore the fact that Bert had no interest in running Denwall or its department stores. He enjoyed crunching numbers behind the scenes.

Will's goal wasn't to prove himself more worthy than his oldest brother of filling Father's shoes, but to earn the infuriating man's trust. Starting with bringing the renovation project in under budget and on time—a minor miracle, at the least.

In a prime location with heavy foot traffic, the view of Denwall from the sidewalk must be top-notch. He removed a handkerchief from his pocket and wiped the glass. His heart sped up as a petite figure with black hair loosely tucked under a wide-brimmed hat strolled by, arm-in-arm with a young man. Will peered through the smudges and dirt.

No, she wasn't Miss King.

The disappointment rolling through him was far stronger than it should be.

He shook his head at the absurdity of his reaction. He'd spent the past five years focusing on nothing but Denwall and his future there. Now, so close to his goal, he was daydreaming of a shopgirl.

THREE

Ivy managed to slip off her boot and found her foot and ankle swollen like a grapefruit. Gran clucked her tongue and insisted on the local druggist's wife, who had a basic knowledge of first aid, to look at Ivy's injury.

"It's not broken," she said as she gently rotated Ivy's foot. "But you sprained it, I'm afraid. I'll wrap it in some bandages. You'll need to stay off your feet for a few days."

Ivy tried to hand the kind woman some money for her trouble, but she waved away Ivy's offer. "It's what neighbors do, and your family has been our neighbor for twenty years."

Unfortunately, although the neighbor was a generous woman, she was also a gossip. Before long, the shop entertained more nosy neighbors than customers, and they came and went until almost closing time, wanting to know all about Ivy's brush with death— as Gran had put it.

"I'm going to put my foot up and do some work in the back," Ivy told Gran when the last of their visitors left the shop. She hobbled to the back and opened the door leading to a small space that served as an office, as well as the hall to the stairs.

After pulling a stool from underneath the desk, she gingerly lifted her throbbing ankle onto the small wooden surface and slid the accounting ledger from the desk drawer. Tallying the day's receipts was at the top of her list of loathsome chores, right after window cleaning.

Dickens pushed open the door with his nose. He padded over to her and gently laid his head in her lap.

Ivy rubbed his head. "Dickens, my boy, my life is a mess." But it hadn't always been like this. She'd come from a happy, comfortable, middle-class family until two years ago when, in a matter of seconds, both Mama and Papa were taken from her.

Now, Ivy and Gran kept the bookshop running to the best of their ability. Other than Ivy's part-time job as a librarian at the Astor Library every weekday morning, it was their only means of financial support.

Dickens moved to his blanket on the floor, and Ivy focused on the work in front of her. With the day's mediocre receipts recorded, she reached over to open the short stack of mail Gran had placed in a wire basket on the desk. On top lay an envelope, and its imagined contents made her insides clench as she slid the silver letter opener—a relic from better days—under the flap. Her eyes skimmed the letter, her worst fear confirmed. In short, their rent would substantially increase in October.

The faint sound of the shop bell caught Ivy's attention, and she glanced at the clock. It was two minutes to closing time, but she would accommodate someone if they wanted to make a purchase. She pushed away from the desk with care and opened the back room door. Dickens moved past her.

The man removing his hat and exchanging pleasantries with Gran wasn't a customer. Ivy's stomach soured like spoiled milk, and she tried to step back before the visitor noticed her, but she moved too quickly and cried out in pain.

"Miss King, are you all right?" Mr. Higginbotham stepped farther into the store. "I understand you took quite a tumble."

Ivy stifled a groan and, behind her, Dickens growled. He didn't like the man from across the street any more than she did. As the owner of an antiquities shop that catered to a wealthy clientele, he'd had few dealings with the Kings over the years. He'd even asked Ivy a time or two for advice on a rare book he was considering bidding on. Sometimes, the man got too close for her liking.

"I'm fine." Ivy's voice came out in an exasperated whoosh, and she loathed to step any closer to the man. "My ankle's just a little sore."

Mr. Higginbotham stared at Ivy for a few uncomfortable seconds and then extended his hand. "You should sit. You have one lame leg as it is." He offered her his hand. "Let me help you to a chair."

Shudders ran up Ivy's spine at the idea of his touch, and she pulled back her shoulders. *How dare he call me lame? I'm not a racehorse.* "I'm fine, thank you."

Dickens sat down next to Ivy as if daring the man to get closer.

"Um, yes, well." Mr. Higginbotham blinked and stepped back. "Did you hear the news?"

Ivy nearly rolled her eyes. The man was an unrepentant gossip.

Unfortunately, Gran took the bait. "No! What news is that?"

"There's a rumor that a department store is moving into the neighborhood. In the old Heinrichs store."

The news explained why the protestors had gathered that morning. Ivy squeezed her eyes shut as dread washed over her. How would they survive the competition moving in just two blocks away? The large emporiums sold books at much lower prices than their small shop could afford.

Without invitation, Mr. Higginbotham walked to the counter and laid his hat on the freshly polished wood. Obviously, he expected to stay awhile.

"I'm about to make some tea, Clarence. Would you like a cup?" Gran beamed.

Since when was she on a first-name basis with him? Ivy glared at her grandmother, who was forever trying to find Ivy a husband,

and their neighbor was an excellent candidate. In Gran's mind, anyway.

He ran a hand over his balding head and preened like a peacock. "My cook is making dinner, and I am expected home soon, but I don't see why I couldn't stay for a cup." He often slipped into conversation that he had a cook and a housekeeper. Admittedly, he did a good business and was fortunate to afford such luxuries.

"Gran, I hate being rude to a neighbor, but my ankle hurts, and I still have some work to do in the back. Can we forgo the tea? I'm sure Mr. Higginbotham understands." Ivy eyed the man and pasted a smile on her face.

He looked as though he wanted to argue but must have thought better of it. "Yes, yes. I understand. Another time." He donned his hat and executed a silly bow. What a fop.

"Well, good day, then." Gran closed the door behind him. "Let's go up and have some dinner, dear," she said to Ivy.

"All right, Gran," Ivy replied, though she wasn't hungry in the least, and followed her grandmother and Dickens, who was always in the mood to eat, up the stairs.

Gran stopped and turned at the kitchen door. "I hope you don't mind having soup three days in a row."

"No, of course not. I love your chicken soup." Ivy's throat tightened with regret and shame. When her parents were alive, they'd never needed to worry about making meals stretch. The bookshop thrived in those days.

While Gran brought their bowls to the table, Ivy stared out the kitchen window, surprised the day had gone by so quickly. Movement caught her attention, and she spotted the newlyweds across the street as they moved behind the filmy curtains of their sitting room window. The husband bent and kissed his wife on the head.

Ivy sighed. She had encountered the couple several times in the past few months. They seemed very much in love.

Gran must have seen them too. "They are nice young people, the Joneses," she said as she pulled out her chair.

Ivy dug into her soup.

"Aren't you going to say grace, dear?"

Ivy's spoonful of soup stopped just short of her lips, but she placed the utensil back in her bowl, too exhausted to come up with words of thanks and praise. "Sorry, Gran. I was woolgathering. Why don't you say grace tonight?"

Gran folded her hands in her lap and bowed her head. "Heavenly Father, thank you for this food and your many blessings, including saving Ivy from disaster today. We pray the Joneses will feel your presence in their young marriage. Amen."

"Amen." Ivy lifted her head and glanced out the window one last time. Yes, it would have been disastrous if she'd been laid up for any length of time. A small part of her conceded that the young bride was fortunate to have a strong man to lean on.

They ate in silence, Ivy's mind churning as she weighed how best to broach the looming issue. In the end, she saw no option but to be direct. "We got a notice this morning—the rent is going up at the start of October. Even with my librarian's job, I'm not sure we'll manage."

Gran's blue eyes, so like Ivy's own, filled with worry. "But what can we do?"

Ivy didn't know. Their last rare book had been sold over a year ago, stripping the store of its former source of income. In her parents' time, the rare book trade had been their livelihood, but without funds to invest in new acquisitions, she couldn't bring in fresh stock. Even if she could, she'd be unlikely to secure a place at estate auctions for such treasures.

Across the table, Gran reached for Ivy's hand. "I wish I could do more." Sadness laced her voice.

Ivy laid her free hand on top of Gran's gnarled one. "You do more than your fair share." Although her grandmother never complained, the arthritis in her hands must be painful. She should be slowing down, not doing more.

When they finished their meal, Ivy stood to clear the table, but Gran waved her back to her seat. "Sit down, girl. You can't clean dishes tonight. I'll clean them in a minute." She laid her napkin on the table. "Why don't I put the kettle on?" Gran thought every problem could be solved with a strong cup of tea.

Ivy preferred to go to bed, but her grandmother seemed to have something on her mind.

Gran bustled around the kitchen, setting the kettle on the stove and removing two teacups from the cupboard. "Clarence is such a nice man. I think he's quite taken with you."

Ivy stifled a groan. She would never have agreed to sit back down if she'd realized where this conversation led.

"You have a lot in common, what with his interest in antique books, and he would be a good provider. If you gave him a sign of encouragement, he would ask you to marry him."

Clarence probably did hope they'd wed. He'd get a mother for his unruly daughters and free labor for his shop. After all, a woman with a limp must be in need of a husband.

Ivy had already turned him down once when he asked her to work for him, to help him ferret out rare, undervalued books he could resell at high margins. However, the salary he'd offered was insulting and even less than the wage she made at the Astor.

"I don't like him, so why would I want to encourage a match?"

After the tea was sufficiently brewed, Gran returned to the table and continued her lecture. "You can't work yourself sick at the shop. You're young. You need to consider marriage and having a man share your burdens."

"Gran, I'm not sure I want to get married."

"Oh, pish. Of course you do. Every woman needs a husband."

Ivy lifted her chin. "There are many unmarried women who do just fine. Look at Zella."

"Your aunt isn't a good example. Besides, I think she's lonelier than she lets on. Losing her husband so soon after they married has just made her skittish." Gran rested a hand on Ivy's. "What about love and romance? Don't you want that for yourself?"

"Romance didn't work out so well for me, remember?"

"Not every man is like him, Ivy."

"Maybe not, but the experience was painful enough. I don't think I could handle that kind of hurt again."

Gran patted Ivy's hand. "You're stronger than you think. Besides, he wasn't right for you."

Apparently, the man she thought she'd marry one day believed that, too, since he'd married her best friend after declaring his undying love for Ivy.

Men often claimed that women were fickle creatures. She begged to differ.

But for all Ivy's bravado about being a spinster and not needing a man, sometimes, in the still of the night, she wished she had someone to lean on.

A knight in shining armor with hazel eyes flitted through her mind. The memory of his arms around her waist made her skin tingle. How gentle he'd been, despite his obvious strength. The warmth in his eyes had made her forget her pain momentarily.

Notwithstanding her self-admonishment, she replayed every second of their brief encounter—the brush of his fingers against hers as he helped her into the carriage. The rich timbre of his voice. The way he'd treated her like she was something precious rather than broken.

She couldn't help but imagine a different life with a man like him.

Ivy shook her head. Dreams were a luxury she couldn't afford.

FOUR

Will glanced at his watch for the third time, pacing the grand foyer of Holland House. He'd asked Bert to meet him for breakfast at eight in the hotel's café to review Bert's numbers before the nine o'clock meeting with the foreman.

Just as he was about to request the front desk staff use the speaking tube system to call up to his brother's room, Bert strolled through the front door, a book tucked under his arm. Will threw his hands up. "There you are! I'd almost given up."

"Sorry. I walked over to the park and lost track of time." Bert removed his hat and ran a hand through his mussed hair. His clothes were disheveled, and given the still, thick air outside, his untidy state couldn't be blamed on Manhattan's weather.

No question Bert was an intelligent man and his memory for facts and figures was infallible. If only he remembered to run a comb through his hair in the mornings. And although the hotel had excellent laundry service, Bert looked like he'd slept in his clothes for several nights. He wasn't unclean, just indifferent to appearances. At least he didn't smell.

"It's getting late. Let's grab some breakfast and head to the store. We've got about an hour." Will didn't wait for a response but strode across the lobby, and his brother followed close behind.

Bert loved to eat, but remembering to do so was another matter. Looking at his lanky form, Will guessed he hadn't eaten regularly since buying his Philadelphia home. He needed staff to help manage his life outside of work.

They found a table by a window in the hotel's popular café, and a waiter took their orders. As always, the service was quick, and the food was hot.

Will hoped the coffee would clear his head.

"All right. What's going on?" Bert set down his cup and glared across the table. "You've been out of sorts for days."

Will sighed and sat back in his seat. "It's nothing. Just anxious about the store, I guess." And proving his worth to their demanding father.

Bert snorted. "You're not the anxious type. Cocky, self-assured, and bossy, yes. Anxious, no. What's really got you in such a contemplative mood lately? That's more my state of mind."

"You read Father's telegram yesterday, didn't you?"

"I did," Bert said.

"He wants the grand opening moved up three weeks. The original date was going to be difficult enough."

Bert shrugged. "We'll do the best we can."

Will pushed aside his half-eaten breakfast. Bert, however, took another spoonful of his steamed peach pudding, one of the Holland House chef's specialty desserts. How could he eat something so sweet first thing in the morning?

Narrowing his eyes, Bert pointed at Will. "What else is going on?"

"What do you mean?" Will shifted in his seat. Bert might forget to comb his hair, but he was astute.

"I can tell you're not sleeping. You've got dark circles under your eyes."

Honestly, Will couldn't blame his lack of sleep on his worry about opening the store on time and under budget. If he were honest with himself, he'd blame his nightly tossing and turning on a blue-eyed beauty who haunted his dreams. He threw down his napkin. "If you're done eating, let's head over to the store."

After signaling a porter to have their carriage brought around, Will informed the hotel clerk they'd be gone for a few hours. They waited on the sidewalk out front and soon their vehicle pulled up.

Inside the carriage, Bert tapped his foot impatiently.

The sound grated on Will's nerves. Besides, they rarely kept secrets from one another. "Fine, I'll tell you."

"I knew you would."

Will took a deep breath. "I told you I saved a woman from falling in front of a beer wagon. Did I also tell you she was beautiful?"

Bert crossed his arms over his chest. "Your foul mood is because of a woman?"

"I can't get her out of my mind." Her smile haunted him. Not the polite one she'd given the cab driver, but the genuine one that lit up her whole face when she'd thanked Will for his service. The memory of her sparkling eyes left him with an ache, a yearning to see her again. Will wiped a hand down his face. "I've tried, but she's in my dreams. As silly as it sounds, I look for her face wherever I go."

"More stupid than silly, if you ask me, since you can see her in the flesh rather than conjuring her up. Didn't you say you know where she works?"

"She indicated it was a bookshop not far from where we met. On Fourteenth Street."

"Fourteenth..." Bert snapped his fingers. "I've been to that bookstore."

Of course, he had. Bert hunted down bookshops like a hound sniffing out a fox.

"What did you say she looked like?" Bert asked.

Will shrugged as nonchalantly as he could. "Black hair. Blue eyes."

A whistle blew from Bert's pursed lips. "I know the woman. She's unforgettable, all right. Smart too." Bert winked. "A first for you." Laughing, he removed his glasses and wiped his eyes. When he finally caught his breath, he continued to grin. "It's about time you were interested in someone other than one of those high-society women you've always gravitated toward." He shuddered.

"Just because I can't stop thinking about her doesn't mean I'm willing to pursue her."

"What are you talking about? You're not committed to anyone else, are you?"

Before answering, Will lifted his eyes to the carriage ceiling and silently counted to three. "All right. Let's say I pursue this woman. Maybe take her to the theatre or share a picnic. Where could it go from there?"

"Hmm. Let's see." Bert paused for effect. "You'd court her, get married, and have five little black-haired, blue-eyed Walraven babies."

Smart aleck.

"Oh, yes. That would go over well with Father. Can you imagine one of us marrying a shopgirl? He'd have a heart attack. No, I'm not risking his health or my future."

───

The bookshop was unusually quiet, even for a Thursday. Ivy wandered around the front room, straightening upright books and polishing the spotless counter. An electric fan whirled overhead, one of Papa's last significant investments before he died. She was grateful for his forethought as the day sweltered like a furnace.

After one last swipe to the counter, Ivy glanced at the handbill a boy had delivered earlier in the morning, inviting booksellers, stationers, and news sellers to organize against department stores. Usually, these groups would hold a meeting where there would be a lot of complaining but little action. Nevertheless, she'd attend—if they'd let a woman in.

The doorbell jangled, and Ivy lifted her head. "Well, hello, Zella. What a nice surprise. I wasn't expecting you today." Mama's younger sister refused to be called *Aunt*, insisting it made her feel old.

Pulling off her gloves and removing her hat from atop her black tresses, Zella walked to one of the shop's comfortable reading chairs and sat with a huff. "This weather is oppressive." She pulled a handkerchief from her reticule and dabbed her neck. "Autumn can't get here soon enough."

Dickens set his paws on her lap and tried to lick her face. Zella sputtered, "Get down, you mangy mutt." When he was sitting at her feet, she scratched him behind his ears and then gestured toward Ivy's feet. "Now that your ankle is doing better, I'd intended to convince you to come for a ride tomorrow afternoon, but after being outside for a few minutes, I'm not sure that's wise. We'll end up prostrate in Central Park."

It was Zella who'd encouraged her to ride. Ivy had shied away from athletic endeavors, but her aunt assured her that she'd be just fine wearing her platformed right shoe and purchased a bicycle for her. Much to Ivy's surprise, she didn't experience the pain in her hips that she did when she walked too far or tried to run.

"Is there a bicycle club meeting?"

Zella waved her hand. "No. Everyone's out of town, visiting the seaside or some other cooler place. Smart girls."

The seaside sounded lovely. Ivy hadn't left the city in years. "I saw your latest article in *The Delineator* about women in China."

"I wrote a similar article about Japanese women for the *Pall Mall* last year, and I guess someone at the magazine saw it."

Ivy leaned her hip against the counter. "It's an excellent article."

Before moving to New York, Zella traveled the world as a wealthy widow's companion. On the side, she wrote extensively about her experiences for various women's publications.

Ivy rubbed the back of her neck, and Zella narrowed her eyes. "You look tired."

"Oh, Zell, business is just awful. I don't know how much longer we can hang on." Ivy pushed away from the counter and paced to the window. "We received a notice this week that there's a hefty rent increase in October. And to top it off, there's rumor of a department store opening up in the old Heinrich building."

Zella stood from her chair and put an arm around Ivy's shoulders. "I can give you some money. It's not much, but it will help."

Ivy shook her head, swiping at a tear that had escaped and rolled down her cheek. Zella had a tidy income from her writing, but it wasn't enough to support three people and a bookshop. Besides, the Kings didn't take charity. "Thank you, but no. I couldn't. And you've already helped tremendously by recommending me to the Astor Library. We'd be in a much worse situation if I didn't have that job."

"That was nothing. You impressed them with your certificate in library science from the Pratt Institute and your experience at the bookshop. From what I hear, they're pleased as pigs in muck to have you." Zella squeezed Ivy's hand and turned to pace the floor. "What about getting back into selling rare books? Didn't you tell me it was once a lucrative business for you?"

Ivy understood Zella's line of questioning. "Yes. Mama and Papa used to attend auctions and estate liquidations together, searching for books to resell. Mama had an uncanny ability to pick undervalued volumes to resell at a tidy profit."

"She was a remarkable woman." Zella's fingers went to the mourning brooch she always wore. Inside was a miniature portrait of Mama, and one of Zella's late husband.

Ivy swallowed past the lump in her throat. "She was."

"As are you." Zella embraced Ivy in a warm hug before drawing back to search her face. "I'm certain you have your mother's ability with rare books. Is it an option for you?"

"It's an excellent thought, just not one I can consider right now." There were too many insurmountable obstacles between her and that dream. She might be welcome in a few auction houses if she had an escort. *Someone like William*, her mind supplied unhelpfully. She could picture him beside her, his strength giving her confidence. But such musing was pointless.

No, there was no potential for an escort, but that was the least of her problems. To build any kind of worthwhile inventory, they needed ready cash. As it was, they barely brought in enough money to keep the shop open.

She patted Zella's hand. "Will you watch the shop for a few minutes while I make tea?"

"I'd be glad too. But I beg you, please don't make it so strong. You may take after your mother in many ways, but your tea is too much like your grandmother's."

FIVE

A dull headache throbbed behind Will's eyes as he instructed the driver to return to the hotel.

His and Bert's meeting with the construction foreman had dragged on for nearly an hour. The man complained about supply delays, permit issues, and a lack of reliable workers. He even hinted at better-paying jobs with fewer problems elsewhere.

"Hold on a minute," Bert said. "I need a new book. Why don't we head over to that bookshop on Fourteenth?"

"There's a Charles Scribner a few blocks from here. Their selection will be better than a small bookshop's." Will knew exactly what his brother was trying to do, and uncertainty gnawed at him. On the one hand, he wanted to check on Miss King. On the other, what was the point? He was in New York for too short a time for anything to develop, and he had little time for anything other than work.

Bert shrugged. "I don't like the big stores. No personality."

"We own some of the largest department stores in the country."

Bert shoved his glasses up his nose. "Exactly."

Five minutes later, they stood in front of a shop with Richard

King, Bookseller, emblazoned across its only window. Was Miss King the bookseller's daughter?

A bell jangled as Bert pushed open the shop's heavy door. Will followed him inside, greeted by the pleasant scent of lemon polish and leather.

Unlike most bookshops he'd visited before, Richard King's shop was well-organized and clean. Shelves of neatly arranged books lined the walls, even behind the gleaming oak counter. Handwritten signs guided customers through the sections, inviting them to browse.

A Saint Bernard wandered from behind the counter and gave Will a sniff.

Near the window, one of two reading chairs was occupied by a striking dark-haired woman who looked enough like Miss King to be related. A sister, perhaps? Her eyes were closed, so he couldn't tell if hers were the same piercing blue.

The store was empty except for the woman. Bert pointed to the far wall and wandered off. Apparently, Will would make the next move.

He removed his hat, ran a hand through his humidity-dampened hair, and stepped farther into the room. His attention turned to a handbill atop the counter. It advertised a meeting of booksellers and stationers. Small shop owners always blamed their woes on the increasingly popular department stores.

Will cleared his throat to get the woman's attention. She opened her eyes—an unusual gray—and sat up straight, a grin on her full lips. "Well, hello there. Can I help you?"

"Good morning. I'm looking for Miss King."

Her finely arched eyebrows rose. "Really? Ivy King is my niece. Is that who you mean?"

This woman seemed too young to have a grown niece, but he supposed it was possible. "I'm sorry. I don't know her given name. I assisted her when she twisted her ankle last week."

"Ah, yes. She told me what happened," she replied, glancing

toward the back of the room. "Oh, here she is now." She waved a hand toward the back of the shop. "Ivy, pet, a gentleman is here to see you."

Will turned, and the breath whooshed from his lungs. This woman was definitely the one he'd met—the woman who'd kept him tossing and turning late into the night. Every night. For more than a week.

His mind hadn't played tricks on him. With ink-black hair curling softly around her face and cornflower-blue eyes sparkling with intelligence and humor, she was as gorgeous as he remembered.

Their eyes met, and she blinked before entering the room to lay a tea tray on the counter.

"Good morning, Miss King." Did she remember him?

"Hello." The word sounded like a question.

Will moved toward her, and the massive dog gave a low growl. Miss King's protector wasn't about to let him get any closer. "I don't know if you remember me..."

She patted the Saint Bernard's head. "It's all right, Dickens." She stepped toward Will and extended her hand. "Of course I do. My knight in shining armor."

A jolt shot to his toes as his fingers touched hers. "I don't know about being a knight, but I wondered how you fared afterward."

"I must admit, my ankle hurt for a few days, but with a little rest, I'm now as good as new." Her lips lifted in a tentative smile.

"I'm glad." He squeezed her hand before letting go, thankful she'd recovered so well. Yet, he was certain he'd seen her favor her right leg when she entered the store. Hadn't she hurt her left leg?

"Thank you for your concern," Miss King said. Two adorable dimples appeared at the sides of her mouth.

Will had never had a problem keeping up a conversation with anyone, male or female, but this woman had him tongue-tied.

Miss King's aunt rose from her seat and stood beside her.

"This is my aunt, Mrs. Capp," Miss King said, her hand on her aunt's arm.

Mrs. Capp extended her gloved hand. "And you are?"

Will dragged his gaze from Miss King's and lightly shook Mrs. Capp's hand. "I'm William Walraven. My friends call me Will." He pointed to his brother, who smirked at him from across the room. "And that's my brother, Robert."

Bert tipped his head. "Good morning." He turned back to peruse the shelves. The rat.

Mrs. Capp tapped her finger against her chin. "Walraven. The name sounds familiar, but I don't think I know any Walravens in New York."

"We're from Philadelphia."

An elderly woman emerged from the back room, her blue eyes an older version of Miss King's.

"Gran, this is Mr. Walraven of Philadelphia. He's the one who helped me when I twisted my ankle last week." Miss King slid her hand through the crook of her grandmother's arm. "Mr. Walraven, this is my grandmother, Mrs. King."

The older woman beamed. "How very gallant you were, sir."

His cheeks warmed at the praise. "It was nothing. I was glad I could be of service to your granddaughter."

"What brings you to New York, Mr. Walraven?" Miss King asked.

Will glanced at the handbill on the counter, deciding not to mention Denwall. "My brother and I are here on business for a few months. Working for my father and his partner." It wasn't a lie, just an omission of details. "We're staying at Holland House."

"Very nice," Mrs. Capp murmured.

"Can I get you a cup of tea? Or perhaps some lemonade?" Mrs. King asked.

"No, that's all right. We should leave. I only wanted to check on your granddaughter's health. Glad to see she's doing well."

"Would you gentlemen like to join us for church services on Sunday?" Mrs. King asked in a rush.

Surprised by the kind offer, Will stared at her and then looked to Miss King for guidance.

Mrs. Capp coughed, and Miss King glared at her grandmother. "Gran, I am sure they already have plans for services."

Will exhaled. Her reluctance suited him fine. He'd come to check on Miss King's welfare. Nothing more. "Thank you, but..."

Bert appeared at his side and cut off Will's regrets. "We'd love to join you."

Will would have words with his meddling brother later. He turned his attention to Miss King. "What time are services? We'll take a carriage and pick you up."

Miss King's face mirrored his own resignation. "Thank you for the kind offer, but the church is within walking distance. The services start at eleven, and we'll meet you there."

"Or you could come by the shop at ten and walk with them," Mrs. Capp supplied.

Wonderful. Another meddler.

Miss King's pretty lips turned down.

Never one to back down from a challenge, Will squared his shoulders. "We'll be here at ten sharp. See you then." He executed a short bow and headed for the door before Miss King could submit a rebuttal.

Dickens blocked the path to the door and lifted his paw. Will laughed and shook it. "Good day to you, too, Dickens."

Six

Blackwing Hall, Pennsylvania

As the matriarch of the Walraven family and wife of Charles Walraven, Laura had spent decades navigating Philadelphia society rules. Yet here in their country house, she enjoyed a more relaxed atmosphere with shorter visiting hours and fewer visitors. People were in better spirits while residing away from the city.

She turned to ring the bell for refreshments, grateful that the days when she fetched the refreshments for visitors herself were long gone. Truth be told, she could probably perform the task in half the time it took the household staff.

On the blue velvet settee across from Laura, her daughter Caroline entertained her guests with the newest French fashion magazine. With Caroline's thick chestnut hair and the Dennison sisters' wavy red tresses, they made a striking trio. The young women oohed and aahed over the newest trends in ballgowns, giggling like the silly teenagers they were.

Laura couldn't imagine any of them married and running a house of their own. She supposed that skill would come with time.

Her two eldest sons...well, she'd hoped by now to be planning a wedding for at least one, if not both.

The Dennison girls' stepmother, Myra, sat in a high-backed armchair to Laura's left. For the past fifteen minutes, she'd tittered on about the latest gossip of Philadelphia society.

Not everyone accepted James's second wife into the bosom of Philadelphia's elite. Still, Laura counted Myra as a good friend, if a little high-strung. What mattered to Laura was that Myra's heart was in the right place. She loved the Dennison offspring as though they were her own family, and Myra could be trusted to keep a secret. If Laura told her something in confidence, she was certain her friend wouldn't blather the information to anyone else—not even her husband.

Myra glanced at the girls and leaned toward Laura. "I heard Elizabeth Blake is still not engaged."

Laura didn't see a need to whisper. "Is that so?" She quirked an eyebrow and took a sip of her lemonade. "But come to think of it, I haven't seen an announcement in the papers." Since the woman threw Will over to marry an English lord, she'd assumed the engagement was a fait accompli.

"If I were William, I wouldn't take that woman back if she begged." Myra gave an emphatic nod.

Laura agreed. Her second son deserved better than that skinny Blake girl, even if it was Charles's wish to unite the two families through marital bonds. What her husband failed to understand was that a marriage needed more than good business sense to succeed. Theirs had been a love match, after all. Yet, with Charles's growing wealth had come a certain snobbery.

Laura, however, wanted her sons to marry for love: to find women who would challenge them and make them better men. They needed someone who could see past the Walraven name and wealth to the man beneath. Elizabeth Blake, with her cold ambition, had never been right for Will. If only Laura had recognized it before her son's humiliation.

Myra set her cup on its saucer with a clink, startling Laura from her thoughts. "How is Charles doing? Is he feeling better now that he's slowed down at work?"

Laura's husband didn't know the meaning of *slow down*. Charles might think he was fooling her into believing that putting someone in as interim head of Denwall would placate her, but he needed to think again. She knew full well that half the time he claimed he was heading to the golf course, he was going to work.

She assumed that was the main reason he didn't put Will or Bert in charge. If they'd taken the reins from him and he still tried to manage Denwall, they'd call him on it—or report it to her.

Maybe I should put my foot down. Demand he put his health as a priority. Besides, she needed to set an example for her children. A wife should be strong enough to stand up to her husband when needed.

"Oh, look at the time, girls." Myra jumped as though she'd been poked by an embroidery needle. "Your father's coming home early today, and he promised to take us to the reception at the museum this evening. We don't want to be late."

"I don't want to go to some stuffy museum," the youngest daughter whined.

"Well, I've given your governess the day off, so you'll have to go to your grandmother's house if you don't come with us."

"Never mind, I'll come with you."

Laura almost laughed at the girl's sourpuss face. She didn't know how blessed she was to have a father who kept a healthy balance between work and family.

Charles had spent far too much of his children's lives at work. He never attended his daughter's piano recitals or rooted the boys on during rowing competitions. To be sure, he loved his children, but he was of the mind that children should be seen, not heard. And when the boys were old enough, they would work—for Denwall. No exceptions.

All three of their sons held part-time positions at the company's flagship store in the summers and after school. After Bert and Will finished college, they went straight to full-time positions. Charles believed they needed to work in every department, learning the business from the ground up. Neither had complained, and both excelled in their own way. Bert was good with numbers and would rather sit in front of a ledger book and create financial plans. Will, on the other hand, enjoyed being with people. He was more of a big-picture thinker and made an excellent manager.

In Laura's humble opinion, both could run Denwall alongside James Dennison if they chose to do so. Bert, however, had no desire to head up the company, while Will wanted the position more than anything. Unfortunately, Charles didn't want to let go. He had used every excuse for not retiring, even though he was ten years older than James, and other men his age and with his wealth had stopped working.

Now, however, he'd been diagnosed with heart issues, and the doctor told him in no uncertain terms to quit working or the stress would likely end his life too soon. Without a doubt, Laura knew Will was the best man for the job. If only Charles believed it too.

SEVEN

Manhattan, New York

"Ivy, dear, it's time to wake up." Gran poked her shoulder.

Ivy groaned and tried to shake the wispy tendrils of a beautiful dream involving a ballroom and a handsome man with chestnut hair. He'd held her close, his gaze warm with affection, her limp forgotten as he guided her gracefully across the dance floor. His touch had been gentle, but sure, his smile meant only for her. The phantom sensation of his muscular arms around her lingered.

Gran poked her for the second time.

Ivy opened one eye to see that the sun had yet to appear over the buildings dotting the street.

Although she'd worked at the Astor Library for the past year, she still wasn't used to the early hours. She was usually up at dawn, but the extra work meant rising earlier.

"Ivy?"

Why was her grandmother so loud? Ivy pulled her pillow over her face. "I'm awake, Gran, no need to shout."

"It's six thirty. Don't you have to leave for the library in an hour? We have some work to do around the shop before you go."

A charming cuckoo clock hung not two feet outside her bedroom, purchased by Mama because she said it could wake the dead. That clock had nothing on Jemima King.

"I'm coming," Ivy grumbled as she sat up and swung her legs over the side of her bed. What she wouldn't give to have one day a week to sleep in.

"I'll get your breakfast," Gran offered.

Ivy summoned a smile. "Thanks." Before Gran reached the door, Ivy added, "Can you make that coffee strong?"

Fueled with oatmeal and the shop readied for the morning customers, Ivy was out the door right on time.

As always, she enjoyed the fifteen-minute walk to the library. This morning, she used the time to reflect on her dream. While her body slept, her mind had created a vivid fantasy of something that would never be, despite her aunt and grandmother's shenanigans. William was obviously a well-to-do man, and she was a struggling bookseller. With a limp.

Soon, the Astor came into view, and Ivy strode toward its entrance. Not for the first time, she admired the grand façade with its classical elements that added a sense of dignity and permanence to the structure.

The library's front doors would officially open at nine and close again at six. Out front, a group of women who also worked the early hours with Ivy stood on the short flight of steps to the library's visitor entrance and waited for the assistant head librarian to arrive and let them in. The women chatted about their lives and their families.

"How's that new husband of yours?" an older woman asked the youngest in their group.

"Oh, he's lovely. I hated to leave our bed this morning, what with him being so cozy and all," the young woman replied with a sigh. Ivy joined in the other women's laughter, but honestly, what did she know about a husband's warmth? Was it really that wonderful?

Mr. Collins—a little man who rivaled Napoleon in ego—arrived at eight o'clock and unlocked the massive front door. "Let's get to work, ladies. No breaks today. The library commission could be by at any time, and since Mrs. Astor might be with them, we want to look our best."

The man was delusional. Mrs. Astor never deigned to grace them with her presence.

"Do you think they'll turn us into a public library, Mr. Collins?" someone asked.

"Oh, goodness, I hope not." Mr. Collins shuddered dramatically. "Imagine all the unsavory characters we'd attract if that were to happen."

Ivy opened her mouth, then swallowed the set-down she'd love to give this snob. Unfortunately, she needed her job and turned her mind to more positive thoughts—like the loveliness of the Astor Library, with its richly frescoed entrance hall lined with marble busts of various classic heroes.

When the women scattered to their duties, Ivy climbed the grand staircase to the second floor. As a library cataloger, she worked at the delivery desk on the east end of the central hall. Before the visitors arrived, she sorted through new deliveries of books from either donations or purchases, recording descriptions, subject analysis, classification, and the authority control designation.

Once the library opened, Ivy organized, shelved, and reshelved books and answered questions visitors might have until she ended her shift at noon. It was reported that the library struggled with financial woes. She empathized with their plight. It was also likely why they hired her part-time. The pay per hour was less than that of a full-time worker.

Like most days, the library was busy. The hum of low voices and the rustling of pages emanated from the rare books' reading rooms. Despite the activity, Ivy's mind wandered, yet again, to William and the Sunday ahead.

She didn't think he'd yet noticed the thick-soled shoe she wore on her right foot. If she stood still, she could cover the unsightly but necessary shoe. However, if she walked, it would invariably peek out from under her skirt.

Would he think less of her when he discovered she'd been born with one leg more than an inch shorter than the other? She dreaded seeing the look on his face when that happened.

The man who she once believed loved her had said her abnormality didn't bother him, but then he married someone who didn't walk with a limp.

Ivy moved around the library's rare books floor to see if anyone needed her assistance. Sometimes people just raised their hands, like they were in a classroom. Some visitors wandered in and out of the various alcoves, while others sat at tables with books already chosen from one of the shelves.

The only way to view books on this floor was with an admission slip, usually assigned by the assistant or head librarian for one month. Upon arrival, the visitors would show their slips to the librarian on duty, and each name was entered into a logbook that was kept at the large oak desk.

Back at the librarian's desk, she ran her finger down the list of names and quickly counted the visitors on the floor. It wasn't unusual for a person to skip the check-in step, but it was her duty to make sure they had permission to be there.

Most of the visitors she'd seen before, and many she knew by name. One man—Jack McGill—scanned the bookshelves. He came in at least once a week, and Ivy assumed he was an upperclassman at a nearby college. Reaching for a thin volume, he glanced over at her, gave her a slight smile, and nodded.

She supposed he was a handsome man in an unconventional sort of way, with dark eyes that stood in stark contrast to his wavy wheat-colored hair. He'd always been courteous to her but spoke little, unlike many of their visitors who liked to chat about their research.

"Excuse me?" A pimply-faced teenager appeared on the other side of the desk. His lips curved in a gentle, self-conscious way. "May I check this book out?" He held out a mustard-colored book entitled *Modern Theory of Heat*.

"That looks like an excellent book for a student." She tried to put the nervous boy at ease. "I assume you're in high school?"

"I'll be starting college in the fall."

"You're off to a good start." She strove for a tone that wouldn't be condescending. "Unfortunately, the Astor is not a circulating library."

Pink rose in the poor boy's cheeks, and he stammered an apology. He started to hand the book to Ivy, and she was sure he would leave.

She didn't take the book from his outstretched hand. "You are welcome to take it to one of our study carrels or reading desks. You'll find other scholars who spend many hours of research here and you are welcome to stay until we close, of course."

The young man pulled the book to his chest and grinned. "Thank you, miss."

Toward the end of her shift, she tidied the shelves and returned books left on the reading tables back to their proper places. Her hand ran over a row of books on the Protestant Reformation, and the books shifted easily under her touch.

Odd.

She usually found this section a tight squeeze.

Something must be missing.

Ivy walked around the tables on the second floor to see if a book or two had been left out. She glanced at the books in the hands of the remaining visitors, yet she found none that could fill the spaces on the shelf. Books *were* missing. She grabbed a piece of paper and a pencil from the librarian's desk and went back to jot down the catalog numbers of the books on the shelf. She opened a drawer of the wooden catalog cabinet and flicked through the cards. Three books were missing.

Ivy stopped the other librarian who worked on the second floor. "There are some books missing. I need to go downstairs and speak to Mr. Collins."

"Oh, that's dreadful," the woman whispered.

"Do you mind keeping an eye on things for a few minutes?"

"No, of course I don't mind. Let me know what he says."

Ivy didn't want to leave the floor with only one librarian for too long, so she moved as quickly as she could to the first floor. Outside Mr. Collins's office, she drew in a breath, and knocked twice on the closed door.

"Come in." A nasally voice called from within.

She opened the door and slipped into the room. "Mr. Collins," she said as she approached his desk.

Mr. Collins lifted his oily head and peered at Ivy through small eyes. He sported a thin mustache that curled up at the ends like two handlebars.

"Shouldn't you be on the second floor, Miss King?" His voice was as greasy as his hair.

"I have Miss Thompkins covering for me for a moment." She pulled the piece of paper with the titles of the missing books from her pocket and laid it on the desk. "I think some of our rare book collection is missing. Perhaps stolen."

Mr. Collins frowned as he picked up the paper.

"As you can see, there are three books from the Protestant Reformation section that I can't locate anywhere on the floor."

He slid the paper into a desk drawer. "I'm sure they've just been shelved incorrectly."

Her back stiffened. To say such a thing implied that Ivy and the four other librarians who worked in that section were inept at their jobs.

"But I'll look into it," he said. "Thank you, Miss King." He bent his head and resumed whatever work he'd been doing when she entered his office.

Clearly dismissed, Ivy turned and left. She suspected Mr.

Collins wouldn't investigate the matter at all. Books often went missing at libraries without ever being returned. Ivy wondered how many of those books, especially the rare antiquities, were stolen and sold to some unsuspecting buyer.

The idea infuriated her.

She returned to her post and kept an eye out for anyone suspicious. What would a book thief look like? No doubt a worm-like man, all slime and slither.

A picture of a man who looked like Mr. Collins popped into her mind.

EIGHT

Confounded, meddling relatives. Why didn't Gran—and Zella, for that matter—just leave well enough alone? Ivy's hands trembled, her nerves as tight as a new book binding, as she slipped into her favorite Sunday dress. A few years old but still presentable, its sleeves weren't as ridiculously puffy as the popular gigot sleeves now favored by fashionable ladies.

The morning sun sifted through Ivy's bedroom curtains, hinting at a gorgeous day. Still, she was cranky. Sleep had been elusive, and she'd tossed and turned all night, thinking about one cleft-chinned William Walraven and the contradictions warring within her.

Every time she closed her eyes, she saw his face. The way his eyes crinkled when he smiled, how his presence seemed to fill the room. Her heart fluttered at the mere thought of seeing him again.

Zella hadn't helped matters. After he'd left the shop two days before, she had filled Ivy's ears with praise for the man. "He's so handsome," she'd gushed. "That thick, wavy chestnut hair. His gorgeous eyes. Why can't I have those eyelashes? It's patently unfair. Did you see that suit?"

Ivy couldn't disagree. William was a good-looking man, yet he didn't appear full of himself or arrogant and didn't put on any airs. On the contrary, he was kind and respectful. Ivy would assume he was an everyday Joe if it weren't for the expensive clothes. Yet they were obviously from different worlds, and he had the power to break her heart—the one thing she promised herself she'd not allow any man to do ever again.

A knock sounded at her bedroom door, and Gran's voice came from the other side. "Zella's here, dear."

Zella? What was she doing here?

Ivy inserted the last pin into her hair and grabbed her hat to head downstairs.

Zella leaned against the counter, looking as striking as a spring meadow in full bloom with her butter-yellow jacket and green skirt. Perched on her head was a jaunty golden-brown straw hat, enlivened with a scarf in cream lace that fell down her back.

"Hello, Zell. What brings you here?"

"I'm coming to church with you."

This was a pleasant surprise.

On second thought, something else was going on here. Ivy narrowed her eyes. "You never join us for church services. Despite my haranguing you."

"Minds can change." Zella stuck her nose in the air with dramatic flair.

"This wouldn't have anything to do with Mr. Walraven, would it?" Ivy stalked to the counter to confront her nosy relative.

Zella reached out and patted Ivy's arm. "Now don't worry, pet, I'm not interested in your man. I'm coming along as your chaperone."

If Ivy had had food in her mouth, she would have spit it out. The idea—all three ideas, in fact—was so ludicrous. "First, I didn't think you were interested in him. Second, he's not my man," Ivy sputtered. "And third, Gran will be with us. Don't you think she is chaperone enough?"

"Think of me as an adviser, then, as I am sure you will give this gentleman the brush-off at your earliest convenience. An act I would vehemently disagree with."

"Says she who will never marry again," Ivy muttered.

"Just because I don't want to marry doesn't mean I don't think you should." Zella moved away from the counter. "Come, Ivy, sit down. Grab a book. Don't look like you're waiting for him to show."

Ivy reluctantly followed her aunt's directive to occupy a chair by the window. Rather than picking up a book, she fiddled with the cameo hanging from a thin chain around her neck. It had been a gift from her parents on her sixteenth birthday.

Glancing at Zella, Ivy frowned. The woman was all smiles and confidence personified.

Ivy, however, was a jumbled mess. Should she have worn her green dress?

The bell above the door jangled, heralding the arrival of the Walraven brothers. The two made a striking pair. They were both tall and obviously athletic, with strong square jaws and the same chestnut hair and hazel eyes.

In their manner of dress, however, they were as different as night and day. William was impeccably suited, his wavy hair cut short without a strand out of place. His face was neatly shaven. Robert, however, had hair that needed trimming, and his clothes, albeit clean, could use a good ironing. Spectacles framed his wide eyes, and a nick on his cheek told of a recent accident with a razor.

"Good morning." William removed his hat. "I hope we aren't too early."

"No. You're right on time, as a matter of fact." Zella stood and approached the visitors. Ivy reluctantly got to her feet and took a few tentative steps, like a prisoner headed to the gallows.

"It's nice to see you again, Mrs. Capp," William said. He sent Ivy a charming smile. "Miss King."

The warmth in his eyes made her knees weak. How did he manage to affect her so strongly with just a smile?

"Hello." Ivy searched her addled brain for something to say. It had been a long time since she'd had a conversation with a good-looking man, let alone two.

"Mrs. King will be down soon, and then we can go," Zella said, filling the awkward silence.

William's eyes searched the shop. "Where's Dickens?"

He remembered her dog's name. That had to be a good sign.

"He's upstairs with Gran. If there's any chance of receiving a treat, she'll be the one to give it to him."

Ivy's gaze shifted from William's face to his brother's. She hadn't realized it before, but she'd seen Robert in the store on another occasion—helped him pick out a book, in fact. A volume on the famous mathematician Carl Friedrich Gauss, if she remembered correctly. "How are you finding the Gauss biography, Mr. Walraven?"

Robert's smile was shy. "Quite enjoyable, thank you."

William made her tongue-tied, and she didn't know what to say to him, but she could talk about books all day. "As a bookseller, it's always fascinating to discover what people read," she said, her curiosity genuine. "What types of books captivate you enough to make a purchase?"

Robert's eyes lit up. "My tastes are varied. I must admit, however, that I've always been enchanted by the allure of rare books."

This wasn't surprising, given the wealthy often collected rare and antique books for their libraries. "Indeed, there's a certain magic in holding a book that has withstood the test of time. The tales they contain, the insights they offer—like holding a piece of history."

"I've found an excellent antiquities dealer and have recently acquired some nice first editions," Robert said.

"Where is the dealer?" Ivy asked, the question stirring a pang of regret. Once, he might have been a customer in their own shop.

"Across the street from Holland House."

"I know the place." They did an excellent business.

"Does your bookshop deal in rare books?" William asked.

His interest in her shop—her pride and joy—warmed her. "We used to. I also work part-time at the Astor Library, so I have the privilege of seeing an amazing collection every day."

"I haven't been to the Astor, but I've heard tremendous things about it," Robert said.

The back room door opened, and Gran stepped into the shop. The brothers both greeted her with charming smiles and gallant bows.

Gran grinned at the attention. "It's such a lovely day. I'm looking forward to the walk."

"I agree," Robert said, pointing his elbow to Gran. "May I escort you, Mrs. King?"

Gran giggled like a young miss and took his arm. It had been a while since Gran had had anything to laugh about, and for that, Robert won several points in Ivy's estimation.

"I'll join you two, if I may." Zella stepped forward and took Robert's other arm. The poor man looked rather alarmed at her boldness.

William didn't offer Ivy his arm. He did, however, walk next to her as they took the lead down the sidewalk. The distance between them was proper, but their arms still brushed and sparks of awareness shot through her each time.

Behind her, Ivy could hear Zella carrying the conversation, and she glanced back to see how the trio fared. Robert's eyes were wide behind his frames. He could be stunned by her aunt's beauty and wit. Still, she suspected he was more stunned by Zella's ability to keep up a constant stream of conversation with a virtual stranger.

The air carried a soft breeze and the chatter of birds. The weather was proving to be cooler than it had been of late. Ivy snuck a peek at the man beside her. He caught the sideways glance, smiled, and her traitorous heart somersaulted.

On the carriage ride to the bookshop, Will's practical mind had argued that this outing with Ivy King was ludicrous. He didn't have time to court a woman in a place he'd be leaving in less than three months. And when he'd walked through the shop door, he found Miss King waiting beside her smartly dressed aunt who epitomized the kind of woman men were drawn to.

But Will's eyes focused solely on Ivy King, and his mind lost the battle with his heart.

Her presence lit up the room. She wore a linen dress that highlighted her cornflower-blue eyes, and her ebony hair, wavy and lush, framed her face with curling wisps.

Walking beside her now, he was once again uncharacteristically tongue-tied. "Nice weather today," he managed to say.

Good job, Will.

"Yes, it's much less humid than yesterday."

As they walked, Will stole a glance at the beautiful woman beside him. Caught, he could only grin. She didn't seem embarrassed but returned the smile.

"How was your week, Miss King?" he finally asked.

She hesitated. "Fine, thank you." Her tone suggested otherwise, but he didn't know her well enough to call her on it. "And you? How goes your business in our fair city?"

"Good. Very busy. It's good to have Bert here." He kept his answer vague. There was time to tell her he was in the department store business. Before she learned this, Will wanted Miss King to get to know him as a man first, not as an heir to a giant emporium.

"You get along well, then, you and your brother?"

Will almost chuckled aloud when he remembered their knock-down, drag-out teenage scuffles. "We do now. Growing up, we were like any other brothers close in age. Extremely competitive."

"Over what?" She tilted her head.

"Our father's attention. Fishing. The last piece of cake."

Miss King's full-throated laugh, so different from the irritating giggles of society misses, delighted him.

"I'm an only child, so I don't know what that's like. But I prayed many times as a little girl that my mother would have a baby."

How sad not to have a houseful of siblings. "Have both your parents passed?"

"They were killed in a train accident on their way to visit a client on Long Island two years ago."

Will remembered reading about a horrific accident that had killed a dozen people. "I'm sorry." Sympathy laced his words. "I can imagine how hard it must be for you." He was at a loss for more comforting words and uncomfortable offering platitudes about a situation he'd never experienced. Despite his tumultuous relationship with his father, he loved him dearly.

And his mother...well, he couldn't bear to think of losing her. She was the glue that held the family together. At least Miss King had her grandmother and aunt.

His arm brushed hers, and he wished he could bring her closer to his side, especially when she peeked at him through those long, dark lashes.

She quickly looked away, and her pace faltered on the uneven pavement.

He glanced down at the sidewalk and caught the tip of a platform shoe peeking out from underneath the hem of her skirt. No wonder she appeared to have a slight limp, even though she'd said she'd recovered fully from her fall.

"My right leg is shorter than the other." The words came out quietly, yet there was a challenge in her tone as if she expected him to cringe.

"I see." She didn't seem like the type of woman who'd want his pity. Instead, he shortened his stride to match hers and met her gaze. "I imagine that's made some things harder for you."

"Some things." The tension in her shoulders eased, and a faint smile curved her lips. "Like dancing. I try to avoid it at all costs."

"That's a shame. It's a skill worth having, and the right partner makes all the difference."

"I might have to reconsider, then." Her voice held a hint of amusement.

"So," he said after a beat, "back to your childhood. Did you compete with yourself for the last piece of cake?"

She laughed, and the sound wrapped around him, warm and genuine. "I never had to. There was always enough for me."

He grinned. "Lucky you."

Their arms touched again, and he tamped down the urge to not only offer her his arm but to protect her.

"Is your family from New York?" he asked.

"No, they lived on farms in the Ohio Valley. Papa always wanted to own a bookshop, and when his father passed, he convinced Gran to sell the farm and move to the city soon after my parents' wedding. Zella moved here about five years ago. She's a writer."

"You and Mrs. Capp are very close."

"We are. She's the only family I have, other than Gran, of course."

"Helped fill the void left by your mother's passing, I'm guessing."

"It did, but not in the way you'd expect. She isn't a mother figure to me, more of a best friend. My grandparents had her late in life, and my parents married when Zella was only seven."

"I've read some of Mrs. Capp's articles," Will admitted.

Ivy's brows rose. "You have? She mainly writes in women's magazines."

Will felt a flush of embarrassment. "My mother and sister have magazines lying about the house, and I've read them a time or two. Your aunt's name is easy to remember."

Pride beamed from her face. "Zella is an excellent writer. Can even make a piece of furniture sound exotic."

Yes, she could.

"What do you do for fun?" Miss King asked.

The question startled him. Fun? He didn't have the time. "I like to play some golf when I can. Go fishing with my brothers." It had been months since they last went to the lake. "What about you? Do you enjoy any pastimes?"

Her lips quirked. "Zella makes sure I get away from the bookshop occasionally. We belong to the Women's Central Park Cycling Club."

That was a surprise. Since she wore a shoe that was thicker-soled than the other, he assumed her disability limited her physical activity. His admiration for her grew at this revelation.

"Do you ride, Mr. Walraven?"

"I prefer horses. My sister Caroline is very keen on cycling, however." He paused and looked at the woman beside him. "In full disclosure, I learned how to cycle so she couldn't hold the inability over my head."

Miss King quirked a smile. "How many Walraven offspring are there?"

"Four. And my mother says that's plenty. Bert's the oldest, then me. Ned is eighteen and starting his first year at Penn in the fall. Caroline is the youngest. She's sixteen."

"The only girl?" When Will nodded, she continued, "She must be spoiled rotten with three older brothers."

Will conjured up an image of his strong-willed yet loving sister. He only appreciated having one once he'd moved out of his parents' home and into his brownstone in Philadelphia. "Yes, Caroline has us wrapped around her finger. But she likes to be treated like one of us and always wants to do what we're doing, especially Ned since he is closest to her age."

"That's understandable. And what is it you brothers do that she wants to participate in?"

"She wants to attend college."

Miss King nodded. "Very admirable."

"And she wants to join the men's rowing team." Will snorted. "Bert and I rowed in college. Ned will too, I'm sure. He also dabbles in fencing."

"Does your sister dabble in fencing too?"

"She did until she realized she couldn't fence well in a dress, and our mother refused to let her wear pants."

"Ah, yes. Several women in our cycling group prefer bloomers, but they're quite controversial." She tucked a stray piece of hair behind her ear. "I still wear the standard skirt."

The idea of Miss King in bloomers almost had Will swallowing his tongue. He imagined she would look lovely in any outfit she chose to wear, although he didn't foresee he'd get the opportunity to find out.

NINE

Ivy had never ventured outside New York, but she always imagined their church, with its grey stone, turret tower, and flying buttresses, belonged in an English village. Despite its location on a busy Manhattan street, the church's abundant grounds and lush trees added to its charm.

The pastor, a rotund man with apples for cheeks and a wide, engaging smile, waited at the entryway to welcome each arrival. Parishioners in their Sunday best filed into the vestibule.

Inside, the nave was filled with the scent of pine and beeswax from a recent polish of the black walnut pews. Stained glass windows cast an ethereal light over the sanctuary, and the voices of the congregants became a low hum as they took their seats.

Ivy followed Gran and Zella to Gran's favorite pew. Warmth surged through her when William slipped in beside her.

As with every Sunday service, not one seat remained empty. Many of the parishioners Ivy had known forever. Some turned in their seats and greeted her with a wave or a tip of the head. When someone tapped her on the shoulder, she twisted to find one of Gran's friends beaming at her from the pew behind. She gave the woman a small wave and faced forward again.

Like all Gran's friends, Minnie seemed bent on seeing Ivy married. The presence of the Walraven brothers would indeed dominate the conversation at Gran's next whist game.

The congregation rose with the calling of the first hymn. Ivy bent to take the hymnal from its rack and bumped into William. He rubbed his head and grinned. She laughed at his exaggerated display of injury and then covered her mouth with her gloved hand when a man in front of her turned and glared.

Ivy counted the song "Meet Me There" as one of her favorites. Surprise washed over her when William's strong baritone sang of the storms of life and the pure and perfect day. To Ivy's right, Zella's sweet voice joined in.

Ivy couldn't carry a tune to save her life, and from the sounds coming from the end of the pew, neither could the oldest Walraven. Still, it felt wonderful to have a handsome man standing next to her, smelling of bay rum and singing like an angel.

The hymn ended, and everyone took their seats. William attempted to fit his long body into the tight space, causing Ivy to take more notice than she should have of how the muscles in his thighs bunched with the effort.

The pastor's likely engaging sermon failed to hold her attention. Instead, she was aware of every movement William made. How his steady breathing made his broad chest rise and fall. How his hands, which lay folded in his lap, were large and his fingers long. That his leg brushed hers too often to be accidental. Much to her chagrin, every occurrence sent a warmth shooting through her.

She squirmed as her mind drifted back to their conversation on the way to church—and the outright lie she'd told when he asked about her week. Shame and fear tangled in her throat at the thought of appearing weak or needy in front of him. No man wanted to be saddled with a burden, she reminded herself. Especially one with much to recommend him.

Although William seemed reticent to discuss his work, she learned that family was important to him. She could imagine him with his three siblings, who probably all looked like him, if Robert was any indication. They seemed like a close family.

How blessed he was not only to have both his parents but to live without financial worries. Of course, this was an assumption on her part, but every sign pointed to wealth, from his clothes to the activities he said he and his siblings took part in.

Ivy wondered, not for the first time since meeting the Walravens, about their family's business and if their mother was the type who'd disapprove of a courtship with a shopgirl.

Will found it adorable that Miss King, who seemed so capable, had a horrible singing voice. But she sang with joy despite the difficulties in her life, endearing her to him even more. On the walk over, they hadn't been alone, but it felt like there was no one else in the world but the two of them.

Standing next to her at church, he felt a sense of rightness. The faint scent of her honeysuckle perfume drifted over him, and he could feel her warmth when they brushed against each other.

The pastor—to whom Will had paid little attention the past few minutes—thumped the pulpit. "Man must live not only by his conscience but also by divine law," he declared, his gaze locked on Will, who squirmed in his seat like a recalcitrant child.

While he hadn't lied to Ivy about his reason for being in New York, guilt pinged at his conscience for omitting important details. Added to that uncomfortable feeling was his concern for Ivy's reputation. From the way other members of the congregation were glancing their way, he suspected Ivy would be the subject of conversation as soon as they left the sanctuary—something he should have considered before jumping at the chance to spend time with her again.

The pastor continued, "Our conscience is a powerful guide,

but it can be swayed by personal desires and rationalizations. Divine law, however, remains steadfast and unchanging. We must strive to align our actions with the higher moral principles that God has set before us. This requires honesty, integrity, and the courage to face the truth, even when it is uncomfortable."

Will's unease grew. No, he hadn't lied, but withholding the full truth about being the son of Charles Walraven, department store mogul, twisted like a knot in his stomach.

"Brothers and sisters," the pastor said, his voice rising with fervor, "we are called to live lives of transparency and right-eousness. Deceit erodes the trust and love that should bind us together, whether by commission or omission. Consider your actions and ask yourself if they truly reflect the divine law we are meant to follow."

Bert jabbed Will in the side with his elbow.

The irony of the situation didn't escape Will. He'd asked Bert not to mention Denwall to the Kings. Just because there was an anti-department store pamphlet on their shop counter didn't mean Miss King had something against his livelihood. Surely, she wouldn't hold it against him. No sense in mentioning it and making everyone uncomfortable.

Chances were, they'd never see each other again.

At the service's conclusion, Will and Bert followed the three women to the church's front lawn—a grassy area where people collected in chatty groups. Miss King was stopped several times and asked about the condition of her ankle. Word of her injury had traveled, it seemed.

Gracious to all the curious parishioners, Miss King repeated the story, including Will's part in the affair. Several nosy ladies gave him the once-over as if to assess his worthiness as an acquaintance of the Kings.

With goodbyes exchanged and the congregation beginning to disperse, the Kings set off toward the bookshop. Will walked alongside the pretty Miss King again as the others walked ahead. Their conversation stayed on light topics such as the weather.

Was it his imagination, or was Miss King putting distance between them? Both physically and emotionally?

Once at the bookshop, Mrs. King unlocked the front door and turned to Will. "Would you care to come in for some tea?"

"No, thank you, Mrs. King." He didn't want to overstay his welcome. Besides, as nice as the last few hours had been, it couldn't lead to anything more. "We appreciate you letting us tag along today."

"We're glad you could join us." Miss King's tone had turned more polite than friendly. "Enjoy your time in New York. Hopefully, our fair city will treat you well."

And that was that. No further invitation. No indication Miss King might want to see him again.

Will tipped his hat with a "Good day."

Their carriage driver, who'd been waiting around the corner, pulled the vehicle next to the shop, and they were soon on their way back to the hotel.

Will let out the sigh he'd been holding.

"Glad to see you've moved on quickly from Elizabeth," Bert said. "She was all wrong for you." He'd never liked her. In fact, Bert tended to avoid society women altogether.

After what happened with his engagement, Will probably should too. "Well, I'm disappointed and more than a little embarrassed about the whole affair with Elizabeth, but I've learned my lesson. I expect it will be a long time before I consider a wife again."

The carriage jostled and edged away from the curb and out to the street. He leaned his head back against the leather seat and closed his eyes. His mind couldn't even conjure a picture of Elizabeth—it was too filled with thoughts of a blue-eyed, ebony-haired bookseller, who apparently had no interest in him whatsoever. But that was fine.

She wasn't his type, anyway.

Honestly, she was better suited to Bert.

The thought hit him like a punch to the gut.

Removing her gloves, Ivy followed her grandmother and aunt into the bookshop. The temptation to watch the Walraven carriage roll away pulled her to the window.

She already regretted her cold and abrupt farewell. In fact, a piece of her heart wanted nothing more than to ask William to join her for a bicycle ride or a stroll in Central Park. But that would be too forward and made no sense for her future well-being. Or his.

Zella threw her hat on the shop counter and turned to Ivy. "So, that's it? You're not going to invite Mr. Walraven back? Even to go to church next week?"

Ivy didn't want to divulge how much she already regretted her decision. "There's no point."

"No point?" Zella's voice was a tad shrill, and she paced the floor. "He's handsome. Obviously wealthy. Nice. And unmarried." She stopped and placed her hands on her hips. "That's the point."

Gran unfolded the Sunday paper and laid it on the counter. She acted as though she was deep in thought over some headline or another, apparently unwilling to enter the fray of this conversation. Unfortunately for Gran, Ivy was on to her. The newspaper lay upside down, and unless her grandmother had skills hitherto unknown to Ivy, she wasn't reading the paper at all.

Ivy strode to the counter and flipped the paper right side around. "William Walraven may possess all the wonderful qualities you have categorized so eloquently, Zella, but it's too late now." Her gaze traveled to the window. "He's gone."

Her aunt wasn't deterred. "Send him a note in a few days. Invite him and that brother of his to dinner or something."

"I couldn't. It would be far too forward." Ivy removed her hat and placed it on the counter beside her gloves. "Besides, what do we really know about these two men? Don't you find it odd that they don't talk about why they're in New York?"

"They're here on business."

"What business?"

"I have no idea." Zella shrugged and let out a breath. "You do have a point, I guess." She sank into a reading chair and cocked her thumb at the window. "I didn't want to mention it, but I tried to get Robert to talk about their work on the way back from church." Her leg dangled over the arm of the chair, and she swung it lightly back and forth. "That man's lips are so tight I'd need a crowbar to open them."

"As I said, odd."

Gran glanced up from the newspaper. "Maybe they don't want to talk about work on a Sunday. It is the Lord's day, you know."

Zella snorted. "Maybe the reason they're so reticent is because they're con men. That Bert looks shifty."

Ivy's lips twitched. Her aunt's instinct for a good story was on full alert. "You've gone from telling me I should ask them to Sunday dinner to imagining them in prison garb. My, what an active imagination you have, Zell."

"Maybe you're right. It doesn't hurt to be cautious. Until we know more about the Walravens, you should steer clear." Zella nodded as if convincing herself that this was the correct tactic.

"They are both very nice young men. I don't think they're trying to hide anything at all, and God willing, we'll see them again soon," Gran interjected.

A part of Ivy wanted to see William again and get to know him better. She'd enjoyed his company immensely. But—and this was a huge but—she didn't want to lose her heart to someone sure to break it. There was no proof, but Ivy was confident Mr. Walraven wasn't looking for a future with a bookseller. A society girl was more his type, no matter what he was up to.

As the day wore on and Ivy was alone in her room, her heart and mind warred. Despite her emphatic declaration to Gran that she had no desire to fall in love, she sometimes wondered what it would be like to have a husband to share the day with, both the joys and the disappointments. Someone to have and to hold, as the vows say. Although she had Gran around her at almost all hours of the day, life could be lonely.

Nevertheless, her mind submitted a strong rebuttal. Too much was already on her plate. She didn't have the time or the energy for a courtship of any kind. Hopefully, the man would vacate her dreams and let her sleep.

TEN

With the demolition of the old Heinrich building completed and deliveries of new lumber and fixtures arriving daily, the rumor that a department store was coming to the neighborhood became a reality. Curiosity brought new patrons to the bookshop, to Ivy's surprise. She appreciated the increase in activity, which kept her from dwelling on William and his absence.

Gran had admonished her for the cold-shoulder she'd given William almost three weeks earlier, and Ivy went back and forth, regretting and applauding her decision to cut him loose. Her mind told her there was no use in developing an affection for the attractive man. She wasn't of his station, nor was her heart fortified to bear the ache of inevitable disappointment.

Still, William's handsome face flitted in and out of Ivy's thoughts frequently, making her smile and setting her pulse racing. Lately, whenever the bell jangled above the door, she'd look over expectantly like a love-sick schoolgirl.

But he never came to the shop. The man was obviously not that interested. Or he showed intelligence and realized a romance couldn't happen between them. She needed to concentrate on keeping her and Gran in their home and their business open.

She shut the cash register drawer. A little girl on the other side of the counter rattled on about the book they'd just purchased as she and her mother headed out the shop door. The mother held the daughter back and told her to wait as Zella hurried into the shop, her face beaming. "Ivy, dear," she said with a flourish of her hand, "we're going to the theatre tonight."

Ivy's momentary joy dissolved when she looked at the work yet to be done. Oh, how she longed to go somewhere—anywhere—different. The theatre would offer a welcome distraction from the daily grind of life, yet she wavered. "I don't know, Zell. I still have so much to do here." She glanced down at the stack of books that had arrived from a publisher earlier in the day.

Zella would not be swayed. "I received an invitation from the wife of one of my publishers." She waved two tickets. "It's for *Trilby* at the Garden Theatre."

Harper's Bazaar had published George du Maurier's popular story as a series the year before. From what Ivy had read in the newspaper, Trilby's themes of art, love, and the power of manipulation translated well to the stage.

Zella slipped an arm around Ivy's shoulders. "I'll tell you what. I'm a quick study. Why don't you tell me what to do? I'll help you finish your work so you can go up and get ready and then have some fun tonight."

With her aunt's help, and if they worked quickly, she could accept the invitation. Ivy pulled in a deep breath and made a decision. "Thanks, Zell. A night at the theatre sounds lovely, although I'm not sure what I'll wear."

Zella lifted a travel bag hanging over her forearm. "I anticipated you might use that excuse not to come with me, so I brought a few things of mine for you to try on. We're about the same size."

Her aunt had excellent taste in clothes, and Ivy tingled with curiosity about what might be in that bag. She'd not worn a new dress in years. Even then, all her dresses were picked for function— to cover her ugly form below the waist. Her boots, made for her by a neighborhood cobbler, were unattractive but necessary to adjust for her right leg.

Theatre gowns didn't go well with her clunky footwear.

"I know what's going on in that head of yours, Ivy King." Zella pointed at Ivy's feet. "You think you can't wear a pretty gown because of your shoes." Her face softened at Ivy's hesitation. "Oh, dear girl, you're more than your boots or those practical dresses you wear. You're clever, charming, and have a light in your eyes that doesn't need silk or satin to shine. Trust me, no one will be looking at your shoes."

Ivy let out a small laugh, and her reservations began to melt. "All right, Zell, you've convinced me. But these dresses better not make me look like a trussed-up pigeon."

"Have faith, pet." Zella's laugh was infectious, and she pulled Ivy into an embrace. "This will be the best night you've had in ages."

Will itched to get started on the remodeling of the new Denwall store. Delays were inevitable, but the situation was ridiculous. They should have started the framing and structural work the day after finishing demolition. Instead, deliveries remained unopened, and workers stood idle.

The barrage of letters from Father didn't offer any support, not that he was surprised. Each missive was laced with impatience, if not outright disbelief in Will's capabilities.

Father's relentless scrutiny was pushing Will to the edge, testing him, making him wonder—was any of this even worth it? But he was a Walraven through and through, and they didn't give up without a fight.

Bert trailed behind as Will pushed through the front door of the building. The clatter of their footsteps echoed in the empty, dusty space.

"We're far behind schedule," Bert grumbled, maneuvering around stacks of new lumber yet to be used.

Will ran a hand through his hair, exhaling sharply. "This project is riddled with one disaster after another. The building commission is throwing its weight around and is insisting on seeing our remodeling plans once more before they sign off on permits. We submitted them, but now they're dragging their feet."

Bert frowned, kicking a stray nail out of his path. "It's not like we're building an entirely new structure. Sounds like a power grab, if you ask me."

"Agreed. But it's irrelevant at this point. We're also behind because we had to find a new foreman after the first one up and quit."

Bert snorted. "Hard to believe there are companies out there paying enough to lure him away."

"That's what I thought." Will suspected a competitor wanting to cause problems for Denwall was behind the resignation.

"But you're happy with the new foreman, right?"

Will moved to the staircase, motioning for his brother to follow. "Very. Bob Owens is top-notch. Speaking of, he should be here. Probably in the subbasement." Descending the stairs, they found Owens busy with some measurements. A short but solid man, he had a nose that looked like it had been broken in a brawl and beefy arms any prizefighter would envy.

"How's everything looking?" Will asked, extending a hand for a firm shake.

"My carpenters are ready to get to work as soon as we receive the okay."

"What about the elevator? Any major repairs?"

"The inspection of the hydraulics proved it was in good shape. The electric lighting and fans are also in good working order."

"At least that's something," Bert said, though his tone carried a lingering irritation.

Will resisted the urge to grind his teeth at his brother's persistent negativity.

Owens ignored the tension in the room. "You still want to install the pneumatic tube system, I assume? We'll need additional manpower since the carpenters will have their hands full.

"That's fine. We'll do what we must." Will wouldn't forgo the system for expediency's sake. The tubes, installed in all Denwall stores, transported cash and sales slips between departments and floors. They were more efficient than using cash boys, reduced theft, and would save money in the long run.

"Understood," Owens said. "If we can start the renovation Monday, we'll finish by the end of the month."

Will sucked in a breath and calculated the shift in time schedules. "That will give us under three weeks to get the shelves stocked and ready for the grand opening on October nineteenth. It'll be tight." His entire family was coming in for the event. He would do everything in his power to make it a tremendous success—and to make his father happy, the most daunting task of all, but the most important for Will's future.

"What about the building commission?" Bert asked.

"I'm familiar with most of the commissioners," Owens said. "I'll work closely with them to ensure the process is smooth."

"Wonderful. I knew you were the right man for the job." Hope —the most he'd had in weeks—glimmered despite the difficulty of the situation. And hope wasn't the only thing lacking in his life lately. Despite only spending a few hours with Ivy King, he missed her. Was that odd?

Little things constantly reminded him of being with her. The scent of honeysuckle or a leather-bound book. A dog barking, and a tinkling laugh. Black-haired women, and particularly ones with blue eyes.

If he saw her again, maybe he'd get over his silly infatuation. As it was, his mind was not on work or returning to Philadelphia in November as it should be, but on her.

Though, to be fair, *infatuation* wasn't the right word. It implied just physical attraction. But he also enjoyed her wit and her passion for books and her shop. He found himself wanting to know everything about her—her opinions, her dreams, what made her smile.

He caught himself wondering what she'd think of his plans for the store's book department. Would she approve of the layout? The idea of her opinion meaning so much to him was unsettling.

Shaking the thoughts from his addled brain, Will motioned for Bert to follow him to the main floor. As they stepped off the elevator, he caught sight of a wiry man, probably in his early thirties and wearing an ill-fitting suit, standing inside the entrance, swiveling his head to take in the dusty room. When the visitor noticed them, he walked farther into the store with a determined stride. "I'm Frank Sage from *The Daily New Yorker*."

Will shook Sage's outstretched hand. "I'm William Walraven. This is my brother Robert. How do you do?"

Sage glanced around the room. "I understand this will be a Denwall Department Store when you're finished."

"That's correct."

"My boss asked me to sit on the story for a while, but I've gotten the go-ahead to run a series on the enterprise." The reporter pulled a notebook from his jacket pocket.

Will wasn't surprised by the information. James had alerted him that *The Daily's* owner was eager to announce Denwall's presence in New York.

Sage focused on Will. "Can you give me a tour while I ask you some questions?"

The reporter's tone was congenial, but Will wasn't fooled. He'd had enough dealings with the press to be on full guard. "By all means." He pointed to some broken slats of wood on the floor. "Watch your step. There's still some cleanup to be done."

"If you'll excuse me, I'll leave Will here to answer your questions." Bert—the rat—made his getaway, leaving Will to handle the interview.

"I understand Denwall paid one and a half million for this place. You didn't get much for your money." Sage tapped his notebook with his pencil.

So, this was how the reporter was going to play the game. "I disagree. It was a fair deal for both parties. We've secured a clear title to all the stock, which was substantial, the fixtures and so forth belonging to Heinrich, and Denwall is free from all claims under adjudication between Heinrich and his creditors."

Sage jotted down some notes as Will led him through the building. "What are your plans for hiring?"

"We'll eventually hire over five hundred employees. Interviews start as soon as the basement is complete.

"Each department will be well-organized and stocked with the highest-quality merchandise." Will showed Sage around the main floor and then took the stairs up one flight. "We also want to make the building inviting from the outside. Each evening, the windows will be lit by over a thousand incandescent lights along the entire storefront on both streets. And each window will showcase expertly arranged merchandise, unlike any other store window in New York."

By the end of the tour, Sage's notebook was filled with scribbles. "I guess that's it for now," he said, snapping it shut.

Will exhaled, relieved the interview had gone smoothly.

However, that feeling didn't last, and Sage's eyes gleamed with a final, pointed question. "What do you say, Mr. Walraven, to the claim that department stores are like octopuses, with their tentacles in the pocketbooks of small shop owners?"

Will had heard variations of this accusation before. His mind went to Ivy's shop, of how he wanted to prove Denwall could coexist with smaller businesses—that he could be worthy of both his father's approval and the respect of a certain blue-eyed bookseller.

"I understand the concern of small shop owners, truly I do," he said, choosing his words carefully, "but my first concern is the customer. Denwall can cut prices and efficiently sell new products by eliminating the middleman and purchasing directly from the manufacturer. This increases the average person's purchasing power here, as well as in markets around the world."

Sage scribbled a few more notes, tapping the pencil thoughtfully against his paper. "I have some other interviews scheduled to add different perspectives to my article. I'm shooting for the article to come out the Sunday after next. Could be earlier."

"Let me know if you need anything more from me." Will escorted the reporter out of the store's front doors.

As the reporter hailed a cab, he turned and handed Will an envelope. "Almost forgot. This is from George Dixon, the owner of *The Daily*."

Will took the envelope and went back inside. The note was short and to the point. He looked up when the elevator dinged. Bert had perfected the art of good timing.

"I have a favor to ask," Will said when his brother reached his side.

Bert pushed his spectacles up his nose. "Why do I feel I'm not going to like it?"

"Nothing horrible," Will chuckled and clapped a hand on Bert's shoulder. "We've been invited to join the owner of *The Daily New Yorker* in his theatre box tonight. Looks like he's also invited someone from the building commission. James thought this might happen. He advised us to accept."

His brother's eyes, so like his own, widened and blinked. "I hate gatherings."

"But you love the theatre." Will could manage the meeting on his own, but it would be easier with reinforcement. "It's important, Bert."

He grinned and gave his brother a light punch in the arm. "Besides, I'm told that our host's wife likes nothing better than to play matchmaker, so there's bound to be some unmarried ladies in attendance."

Bert's eyebrows rose, clearly intrigued. He may be quiet and introspective, but he still enjoyed the company of a pretty woman. "To the theatre it is."

ELEVEN

Will slipped his arms into his black, satin-lapelled jacket and adjusted his tie in the mirror. The invitation for drinks in the Holland House bar lay atop the mahogany console in his hotel room. Tonight promised a long evening, with dinner following the theatre, as was typical for such functions.

These society events were opportunities to prove himself worthy of being at the helm of Denwall, but sometimes he wished for simpler pleasures—like spending time with a certain blue-eyed bookseller.

After a final glance at himself, he headed to the first floor, opting for the elevator instead of the stairs he usually preferred. The lobby was bustling, and with no sign of Bert, Will crossed the marble foyer and stepped through the doors into the lively bar.

"May I help you, sir?" The maître d', a tall man with a prominent nose, greeted him at the entryway.

"I'm William Walraven," Will replied.

"Ah, yes. Mr. Dixon is waiting for you. Right this way."

They navigated through groups of men seated at round tables. The room was softly lit and filled with the low hum of conversation. Will caught snippets of discussions ranging from politics to sports. The woodsy scent of cigar smoke permeated the air, adding to the bar's convivial atmosphere.

In the far corner, Will spotted an imposing man with a thick, well-trimmed beard and mustache. As he approached, the man rose from a red velvet armchair.

"Mr. William Walraven, sir," the maître d' announced.

"Walraven." The man extended his hand, his grip firm and confident. "I'm George Dixon."

"Glad to meet you. Please, call me Will." Dixon was a few inches shorter, with salt-and-pepper hair neatly combed back from a broad forehead. His piercing blue eyes scrutinized Will with a keen, assessing gaze.

James had mentioned Dixon's impressive rise from a cub reporter to a successful newspaper owner. Known for his instinct to spot trends and take calculated risks, Dixon had acquired a struggling paper and transformed it into a profitable venture.

Dixon motioned to a chair across from him. "Have a seat."

The maître d' hovered nearby. "What can I bring you, sir?"

"Just a soda water, please."

Will settled into the chair opposite Dixon, his back to the room.

"One of the city's building commissioners will join us at the theatre later." Dixon's eyes shifted over Will's shoulder. "Ah, this must be your brother."

Will turned to see Bert approaching the table, looking uncharacteristically neat in a black coat and tails. He could look rather dapper when he wanted to.

Bert extended a hand to Dixon. "Bert Walraven."

"Nice to meet you. Dennison and I go way back, and he's told me quite a bit about you two."

Bert's eyebrows lifted in mild surprise. "Not sure if that's a good thing."

"On the contrary, he's very complimentary."

A waiter arrived with the drinks, and Dixon sipped his

Manhattan, a blend of whiskey, sweet vermouth, and bitters. He reclined in his chair, his gaze steady on Will. "My editor-in-chief mentioned one of his best journalists is on the story, but I'd like to hear about your plans for Denwall."

Will spent the next few minutes outlining their enterprise and the challenges they faced, particularly the building commission's reluctance to sign off on essential permits.

Dixon's brow furrowed. "Not surprising. You aren't the only department store in the city. Some of your competitors have formidable connections. They've likely exerted influence on the commission to slow your progress."

"That they have." Will labored not to reveal his frustration.

"Well, you'll have a chance to speak with a building commissioner tonight. He's fair and might be persuaded to encourage the commission to expedite things."

Will raised his glass. "That's the goal." Although he knew persuasion sometimes involved money under the table, he'd not stoop that low. Words of reason, and the benefit a store like Denwall would bring to the neighborhood, would have to suffice.

"We appreciate you inviting him tonight," Bert added.

"Glad to." Dixon checked his pocket watch. "We should head out. My wife despises it when I arrive after the curtain call." He signaled the waiter. "Put this on my tab and have my carriage brought around, please."

"Right away, Mr. Dixon," the waiter responded with a bow.

Will and Bert followed Dixon out of the bar. They retrieved their hats in the lobby, where elegantly dressed couples milled about, ready for a night on the town. Outside, a line of carriages awaited passengers.

"Here we are." Dixon tipped his head toward an open barouche drawn by two handsome chestnut trotters.

Will and Bert climbed in, taking the seat across from Dixon. As the carriage rolled into the busy street, Dixon cleared his throat, a hint of amusement in his eyes. "I should warn you. My wife fancies herself a matchmaker. She was delighted when I mentioned two young, unmarried gentlemen would join us."

The seat beside Will creaked as Bert shifted uncomfortably. Will glanced at his brother, who was running a finger under his collar, clearly uneasy. The brothers were well aware of the influence society matrons could wield, orchestrating courtships with the precision of seasoned puppeteers.

Will felt no stir of interest at the prospect of eligible females. Lately, he found himself comparing every woman to Miss King, and none measured up. Her genuine warmth and quick intelligence had spoiled him for superficial society matches.

"Oh, and my two lovely, unmarried daughters will also be in attendance." Dixon's eyebrows waggled.

"Good grief," Bert muttered under his breath.

Dixon chuckled, his sharp ears missing nothing. "Don't worry, I won't hold your feet to the marriage fire." His expression grew serious. "Unless there's cause to."

Message received.

Ivy stood at the bookshop window, her white-gloved hands running over the silk shawl she wore. One of her mother's favorite fans hung delicately from her wrist.

She glanced at her feet. Her Sunday shoes—custom-made, like her everyday boots—gleamed in the light of the nearby lamp. While Ivy dressed, Gran had polished the black leather until it shone like new.

"I'm sure your aunt will be here any moment," Gran's soothing voice came from behind. "You know what they say about a watched pot."

Ivy turned, giving her grandmother a small smile. "I'm just a bit excited and nervous, I suppose."

"That's perfectly natural, but I assure you, you look lovely."

"I don't want to embarrass Zella in front of her friends."

Gran moved to stand beside Ivy, slipping an arm around her waist. "You'll be fine. Your mother raised you to be a lady, and you're smart. Just because you can converse on many topics doesn't mean you're too outspoken."

Ivy was thinking more of her ungainly walk, which even the shiniest of platform shoes couldn't completely fix. The fact that Gran would mention her penchant for forthright speech, however, made her lips twitch. "You would say that. After all, I take after you."

Gran laughed and pointed to the window. "There's your aunt now."

A carriage pulled up to the sidewalk in front of the shop.

Ivy took a deep breath and let it out in a rush. "Well, I'm off. Wish me luck."

Gran enveloped her in a hug. "Have a wonderful time, dear. Remember, you're a work of God's hands. Perfect, just as you are."

Outside the shop, the driver greeted Ivy and hopped down from his perch to open the carriage door. "Evenin', miss."

"Good evening." Ivy lifted the skirt of her gown and carefully stepped into the carriage.

"You look splendid," Zella exclaimed as Ivy settled into the seat across from her aunt. "I knew that dress would suit you perfectly."

Ivy smoothed the deep-apricot taffeta silk gown. "It's lovely. Thank you for lending it to me." She admired her aunt's elegant black satin dress draped in brocaded chiffon.

The carriage wheels squeaked as the horses clip-clopped along the brick-covered streets. Anticipation hummed through Ivy's veins. When her parents were alive, and Ivy was of age, they'd attended the theatre often, although not in the expensive boxes they'd be seated in tonight. "Do you think the theatre will be busy?" The prospect of an imposing crowd made her hands tremble.

"Most assuredly. *Trilby* is the only show in town, especially with most of the country-house crowd not returning for at least another week."

"Why aren't our hosts in Newport or wherever the wealthy spend their summers?"

"George Dixon doesn't like being away from the city for too long. He always says that news doesn't take a vacation."

"And what about his wife?"

"She was in Newport for a few weeks but enjoys her husband's company, unlike many of their set who prefer the social whirl."

"It was generous of her to invite you."

"We became fast friends after George introduced us. She comes from humble beginnings, and she and George met long before he became wealthy. I think you'll like her, but I must warn you, she has a penchant for matchmaking."

Ivy groaned and looked out the window. She doubted anyone at such a grand event would find a shopkeeper interesting. Her hands twisted in her lap as the theatre marquee at the corner of Madison and Twenty-seventh Street came into view. Carriages lined the street, and theatregoers packed the sidewalk. All were elegantly dressed and ready for the night's entertainment.

"We're here," Zella announced as their cab came to a stuttering stop.

Ivy slipped her reticule over her arm and adjusted the silk shawl around her shoulders. The driver opened the door, and she alighted, taking extra care to avoid stumbling in front of the fashionable crowd.

Once on the ground, she looked up, admiring the stately Italian Renaissance-style building with its buff-colored brick and terra cotta ornamentation.

The doors opened promptly at eight, and Ivy followed her aunt through the bustling lobby. Zella exchanged greetings with a few patrons, and a doorman ushered them through the inner doors to the auditorium.

While the theatre's exterior exuded Italian elegance, the interior was a sparkling homage to Louis XVI, from the plush crimson chair coverings to the stage's drop curtain depicting a Versailles landscape. The dome above the audience was adorned in white and gold relief, and striped silk draped the walls. The stage was low enough for those in the first row to have a perfect view, and every seat in the house offered a good vantage point.

Ivy trailed Zella through narrow corridors and upstairs to the luxury boxes flanking the stage. What would the people who could afford such luxuries be like? Would they simply ignore her or whisper catty remarks?

The mingled scent of ladies' perfume and fresh-cut flowers permeated the air as they reached the top tier. An usher directed them to the Dixons' box, where several men and women chatted gaily. Some were already seated, while others bent over the balcony railing, observing the theatre below.

"Mrs. Capp, there you are," one of the women called out.

"Mrs. Dixon, thank you for inviting us." Zella turned slightly, placing a hand on Ivy's arm. "Allow me to introduce my niece, Miss Ivy King. Ivy, this is my dear friend, Mrs. Dixon."

Mrs. Dixon clasped Ivy's hand warmly.

While Zella and her friend conversed, Ivy stood slightly to the side. Tall and graceful, Mrs. Dixon exuded an air of elegance, her silver-streaked hair expertly coiffed and her bright green eyes sparkling with sincerity. Despite her wealth, she projected an approachable demeanor that put Ivy at ease.

As new arrivals entered the box, Mrs. Dixon excused herself. Ivy and Zella found two seats in the front row by the balcony. Ivy leaned forward, peering through the railing at the crowd below as patrons found their seats. A petite woman wore an enormous hat resembling a nest with a decorative sparrow perched on top. Ivy stifled a giggle, wanting to point out the absurd millinery to her aunt when she caught sight of a tall man in the passageway outside the dimly lit enclosure.

Her breath caught in her chest.

It was him—unmistakably him—with that air of confidence and elegance wrapped in perfectly fitting evening wear.

Although she hadn't seen him in several weeks and figured she never would again, the swirl of emotions was undeniable. Her hands, still gripping the balcony railing, grew clammy inside her gloves. And her heart betrayed her resolve to forget William Walraven.

TWELVE

The drive to the theatre had given Will time to shore up his arguments for the city building commissioner. Convincing the man of the importance of moving forward with Denwall's remodel was critical. A dormant structure did no one any good, whereas an active project brought jobs and, eventually, money into the community.

The rocking carriage lulled Bert into a doze shortly after their departure from the hotel. Mother always said Bert could sleep in a tree if necessary. When they arrived at the theatre, Will had to nudge him awake, and Bert trailed behind as they made their way to Dixon's theatre box. Knowing his brother, Bert was probably taking in the opulent surroundings. Hopefully, he hadn't crashed into another attendee.

In the passageway outside a row of several theatre boxes, George Dixon stopped to greet a tall woman, kissing her on the cheek. "Dearest, this is William Walraven."

Mrs. Dixon's smile reached her keen green eyes. "It's wonderful to meet you." She waved a hand at the boxes behind her. "We are fortunate to have two boxes this evening: ours and the one next to us. The Crenshaws are still in the country, so we procured their tickets."

Her tone turned shrewd. "I hope you don't mind, but since you are unfamiliar with our guests, I've decided to choose a box for you." When Will quirked a brow, she continued. "Don't worry, Mr. Walraven. There will be plenty of opportunities at dinner to discuss business."

Will didn't argue with the formidable woman and allowed her to show him to his designated box.

Beyond the curtain, several people were already settled.

Mrs. Dixon shifted closer and whispered, "This box is mainly younger people like yourself, including my daughters."

Let the matchmaking commence.

Will grinned, shaking his head in wonder. Mrs. Dixon's strategizing was commendable. She should have been a commander in the army.

"I won't presume to tell you which seat to take." She turned, her eyes drawn to something over Will's shoulder. "Ah, this must be the other Mr. Walraven. Robert, I believe."

As Bert and Mrs. Dixon got acquainted, Will slipped into the box. Two tall women who resembled the hostess stood in the corner of the box behind the chairs, chatting with a young man who seemed pleased with the attention. Will glanced around to find a seat when his gaze landed on a woman in a shimmering apricot gown in the front row who stared at him over her shoulder.

Ivy King.

And, if he wasn't mistaken, the other woman with her back to him was her aunt, Mrs. Capp.

A jab in his ribs caused Will to swivel his head to the left. Bert smirked like the cat who'd caught the canary. "Isn't that Miss King?"

His brother knew good and well it was. Bert might have poor eyesight, but the woman's ink-black hair and bright blue eyes were unmistakable.

Bert started to move around Will. "There's a place open next to her. I think I'll take it."

Will's hand shot out and gripped his brother's arm. "Not on your life."

Bert's chuckle was low as Will wound his way through the chairs.

"Good evening, Mrs. Capp, Miss King." He executed a slight bow.

Mrs. Capp's lips widened in a smile. "Mr. Walraven, what a surprise."

Even in the dim light, he could see Miss King's cheeks flush. "Good evening, Mr. Walraven." Not rude, yet not welcoming, either.

"May I?" Will indicated the spot on the other side of Miss King.

"Of course," Mrs. Capp answered. "We'd love to have you join us, wouldn't we, Ivy?"

Miss King mumbled something he couldn't make out, but she moved her legs so he could pass in front of her. The seats in the boxes weren't permanent, like those in the auditorium below, but comfortable armchairs that could be rearranged if needed. He pulled the chair slightly closer to Miss King.

"How have you been?" Will asked once she greeted his brother. It rankled that her demeanor was less guarded with Bert.

She turned ever so slightly in her seat. "I've been well, thank you. And you?"

"Fine. Busy."

Business was the last thing he wanted to talk about. For more reasons than one. Instead, he had the insane urge to lean in and whisper that she looked lovely. Would she welcome the compliment?

Before he could give in to the impulse, the lights in the auditorium dimmed, and the opportunity slipped away.

As the curtain rose, the anticipation in the air was palpable, mirroring the emotions swirling within Ivy.

She squirmed, and when her skirt brushed William's leg, she froze and tried to concentrate on the story unfolding before them.

Ivy's jaw almost hit the floor when he'd moved from the passageway to their box earlier. Not that she had any preconceived notions of who might be in attendance, but she hadn't imagined this scenario. Yet here she sat, her heart palpitating and her mouth dry.

She hadn't had this sort of reaction to a man since her class-mate at the Pratt Institute, which hadn't gone so well for her. His equal in social status, yet she still wasn't good enough to hold his interest for long. Not pretty enough to marry.

Even then, the attraction she'd had for that man, who she'd thought she loved, was nothing compared to how William's presence drew her.

Stop! This is no good. She needed to guard herself against the onslaught of emotions he aroused.

Ivy bent forward, focusing on the stage as its depiction of a bustling Paris street came to life. Unlike William, who'd likely visited such places as the wealthy often did, she'd never set foot in Paris. Yet, the scenes on stage captured her imagination, making her feel as though she'd strolled those cobbled avenues herself.

The story revolved around the captivating Trilby and her entanglement with three artists who adored her in their own ways, especially Svengali, the gifted pianist and composer with a haunting charm. As Trilby's life intertwined with theirs, she slowly changed under Svengali's eerie, entrancing influence—a shift that had Ivy clinging to the edge of her seat. She couldn't help but feel for Trilby—a pure, impressionable young woman swept up by forces beyond her control.

Ivy stole a glance at William, feeling both thrilled and nervous to be beside him in such an intimate setting. Despite the riveting performance, every fiber of her being tingled because of the man next to her. The scent of bay rum, and his chiseled jaw as he concentrated on the stage. The heat emanating from his arm through his jacket. The way he stretched his long legs in front of him in an apparent effort to get comfortable. His hands, with their long fingers, rested in his lap. The way he sat forward, just a little, during the most intense scenes.

Ivy gave full credit to the performance because the house lights came on for intermission before she knew it. Skirts rustled, and chairs creaked as patrons chatted with their neighbors, some taking the chance to get a refreshment or visit the lavatory.

"What did you think of the performance so far, Miss King?" William asked as he twisted his chair toward hers.

Ivy couldn't hide her enthusiasm. "It's so many things. Suspenseful, captivating, sad."

He chuckled and quirked an eyebrow. "Yes, but are you enjoying it?"

"Immensely. I read the series last year but seeing it on stage brings so much more depth to the characters. Especially Svengali."

"Does it follow the series well, do you think?"

"You didn't read it?"

"No, but my brother did." He pointed his thumb in his brother's direction.

Ivy turned to find Zella gesturing at the stage and talking simultaneously. The quiet-natured Robert Walraven stared, blinking every so often like a spectacle-wearing owl.

"Your brother is quite laconic," she said.

"He's more of a thinker, our Bert. However, engage him in conversation about books, and he'll talk your ear off."

She smiled. "Well, if anyone is up to the task, it's me."

William's jaw clenched, and Ivy wondered what had annoyed him.

"Are you having supper with the Dixons after the performance?" she asked, more curious than she should be.

He nodded just as the house lights dimmed for the final act.

Ivy contemplated who he'd be seated by in the coming hours. If Mrs. Dixon was indeed the matchmaker Zella said she was, William would surely be placed with one of the hostess's lovely daughters at dinner. Relief and envy warred within her.

From time to time during the second act, she felt William's eyes on her, and her cheeks flushed with a mix of embarrassment and delight. Could he sense her unease?

As the plot unfolded, the dynamic between Trilby and the mesmerizing Svengali held Ivy's attention. She couldn't help but draw parallels between the characters on stage and her contradicting feelings toward William. The struggle of wills and the undeniable pull of attraction. And when the play reached its poignant climax, she caught herself leaning closer to him.

He turned to her and smiled, and their faces were mere inches apart.

Willing her cheeks to stay cool, she pressed her lips together, steadying herself against the sudden rush she could only hope didn't show on her face.

In the final scene, tears welled up in Ivy's eyes at the sorrow and redemption playing out onstage. As the curtain fell and the lights slowly brightened, she took a deep breath, trying to steady her racing heart.

William turned in his seat, and their gazes caught, each searching the other's face. Something in his eyes told her he'd been as moved by the story as she.

The audience erupted in thunderous applause at the final curtain call, and everyone stood and made their way to the back of the box.

William clasped Ivy's hand before they moved into the aisle. "I'll see you at dinner."

Unfortunately for her, she anticipated it more than anything else she'd ever looked forward to.

Thirteen

Their hostess insisted Ivy and Zella join her in her opulent carriage for the drive to the Dixon residence on Fifth Avenue. Mrs. Dixon and Zella spent the time conversing about the enthralling play they'd just attended.

Ivy seated herself across from the Dixon daughters and Miss Lippincott, a vivacious young woman whose family rode in their own vehicle. The three young women chattered like excited magpies. Ivy listened with half an ear while she stared out the window.

"Isn't Mr. Walraven a dream?" one of the women sighed.

"Which one? They're both utterly dashing."

"I think I prefer the more talkative one. William, isn't it?"

Ivy's folded hands clenched at the name. She wished these silly girls would find another topic of conversation.

"Yes, that's right." The youngest Dixon daughter placed her gloved hand on her chest with dramatic flair. "But there's something about Robert that makes my heart flutter. He's so brooding. A poet, no doubt."

Next to her, Zella nudged her arm, and she shook in quiet humor.

The carriage rolled through the luxurious Upper East Side, not far from Central Park, until it stopped in front of a towering four-story mansion. A light-colored limestone home, like many in the area, it boasted a profusion of garlands and scrolls. Rows of giant columned French windows stood proudly beneath a mansard roof.

A footman in splendid livery stepped up and opened the carriage door. The six women poured out of the carriage with surprising grace. Mrs. Dixon ushered them through majestic oak and iron entry doors into the palatial interior, where they handed their stoles to waiting maids.

The entryway alone rivaled the size of the Kings' entire apartment. Ivy suppressed the urge to twirl, absorbing the grandeur from the gleaming granite walls to the polished marble floors. An enormous crystal chandelier cast an ethereal glow on an intricately carved round mahogany table showcasing a stunning milky white and cobalt blue Ming Dynasty vase. Or an impeccable replica.

"Dinner will be ready shortly," Mrs. Dixon announced. "Until then, we'll join the gentlemen in the salon." Her voice resonated with authority as she ascended an impressive sweeping granite staircase. The women traipsed behind, their shoes tapping on the parquet floor.

Ivy's hand ran along the carved banister as she made her way upstairs. She stepped into an enormous room, and the scent of aged wood and fresh-cut flowers tickled her nose. Velvet drapes in rich hues framed the windows, a sharp contrast to the simple fabrics in her home.

What would it be like to live in this house? To wake up every morning and not have to worry about how to pay the bills or make meals stretch? Did these people realize how blessed they were?

Laughter and the clinking of glass resonated through the room as guests mingled in animated clusters. Mr. Dixon beckoned Zella to join in conversation with the Lippincotts. Ivy moved to sit next to the youngest Dixon daughter. Her fingers brushed the luxurious brocade fabric of the settee as she surreptitiously glanced around the room.

William stood by the fireplace, an amber-colored drink in hand, conversing intently with a man introduced to her as a building commissioner.

Robert, who must have been waylaid elsewhere, entered the room. Miss Dixon raised her hand, and a delighted expression crossed her face. "Mr. Walraven, come join us." She patted the spot beside her on the settee.

He looked momentarily befuddled but recovered admirably, choosing instead to sit in an armchair that flanked the settee.

Smart man.

Miss Dixon's mouth drooped, but she recovered with the poise of someone well-trained in being a gracious hostess. "How did you enjoy the play?" she asked, her tone vibrant with curiosity.

"It was quite good. And you? Did you like the performance?" Robert responded with polite interest.

Miss Dixon shuddered dramatically. "Svengali was so terrifying. What horrid eyes!"

Robert's hazel eyes blinked behind his spectacles, a hint of amusement flickering in their depths.

Ivy coughed, attempting to dispel the awkward silence. "So, Mr. Walraven, have you purchased any books for your collection recently?"

Robert shifted toward her, and his eyes sparkled. "Yes, I did, as a matter of fact. I recently acquired a first edition set of *Robinson Crusoe.*"

An impressive purchase, indeed. "All three volumes?" When he nodded, Ivy's curiosity deepened. "That is a splendid addition to any library. What kind of binding do they have?"

"All are perfect and unwashed, uniformly bound in full brown morocco, with gilt edges and center ornaments on the sides."

The volumes sounded suspiciously like the collection she'd

recently seen in the rare books room at the Astor Library. Ivy hesitated before asking, but curiosity got the better of her. "Did you buy the set at the bookshop near Holland House?"

"No, I purchased them from a young man—a scholar—I met outside the shop who said he'd tried to sell them in the bookshop, but the owner wasn't in the market for Defoes. The poor man was in dire straits and willing to sell them for much less than they were worth."

Ivy understood the difficult circumstances that could lead one to sell a beloved book. She'd done so herself just a year ago. Still, this smelled fishy. As soon as she had the chance, she'd check the Defoe books at the Astor.

Books frequently went missing from libraries such as the Astor and the Lenox. Some were probably stolen while she was on duty. With all the people coming and going, little security staff, and only one or two librarians on each floor per shift, stealing a book wouldn't be difficult. The libraries often didn't know for days or even weeks that a book was missing, and stolen books were of low priority to the police. When these types of criminals were caught— which didn't happen often—they received little to no punishment.

Because of the low risk of punishment and the high reward of absconding with a valuable book, Ivy wouldn't be surprised if book thieves returned over and over to the same library to commit their crimes. She might even know them by name. The thought jolted her. She placed a hand on Robert's arm. "What did this man look like? The one who sold you the Defoes."

Without hesitation, Robert replied, "He had blond hair and the darkest eyes I've ever seen. They seemed to look right through me."

The description sounded a lot like one of their frequent patrons, Jack McGill. But she couldn't go around accusing someone when she hadn't witnessed the theft or the sale of the books to Robert. Besides, Mr. McGill could be an innocent party.

Before Ivy could ask any more questions, the butler entered the room and spoke in quiet tones to the hostess.

"Let's move into the dining room, please," Mrs. Dixon announced, her voice commanding attention.

George Dixon ushered an elderly woman from the parlor, followed by the other guests, moving two-by-two like a procession of nobility.

Robert charmed Ivy by standing and extending his elbows to her and Miss Dixon. "Shall we?"

⊹───⊱⊰───⊹

Will stared as Bert escorted Ivy—he thought of her that way, even though she'd not permitted him to call her by her given name— from the grand salon. Jealousy flickered in his gut. Bert and Ivy had been in deep conversation for the past fifteen minutes, and Will longed to join them.

Not that his time had been wasted. On the contrary, he'd convinced the building commissioner that granting the remaining permits to Denwall would benefit the city. Employment and neighborhood growth, he argued, outweighed the whims of those powerful enough to delay the inevitable.

"There you are, Mr. Walraven." Mrs. Dixon's voice broke through his thoughts. She looped her hand through his arm. "Have you met my oldest daughter?"

Will shook his head. He hadn't had the opportunity at the theatre.

"I would appreciate it if you would escort her to the dining room."

The efficient Mrs. Dixon wasted no time pairing the young men in the room with available women. He thanked his lucky stars she hadn't paired him with Miss Lippincott, who seemed to revel in vicious gossip.

Mrs. Dixon guided him to the window, where a tall woman with ginger hair and impeccable posture stood gazing at the darkening sky.

Miss Dixon turned and politely held out her gloved hand. Will gave her fingers a light squeeze. Under other circumstances, Will might find her the perfect companion, someone he'd like to know better. Unfortunately, a beautiful bookseller had his full attention.

"My mother says you're from Philadelphia, Mr. Walraven," Miss Dixon said as they walked from the room and into the hall.

"That's correct."

"What brings you to New York?"

"My family is expanding its business here, and my brother and I are heading the project."

"And what business is that?"

Will hesitated. He realized Ivy would soon discover his reason for being in New York but hoped it wouldn't be tonight. Nevertheless, he doubted she could hear him from the dining room. "We own Denwall Department Stores. We're opening our first New York store."

Miss Dixon's eyebrows rose. "Department stores. Interesting."

"Our grand opening is in the middle of October, God willing. Right before the holiday season shopping begins."

In the dining room, Will and Miss Dixon took the seats to Ivy's left. The arrangement staggered the female and male guests, allowing him to sit beside Ivy. Tired of Bert monopolizing her, he gave himself a mental pat on the back for his good fortune.

A silent servant poured wine into the elegantly cut crystal at their right hand. Oysters were served first, but Bert put up his hand. "None for me, thank you."

"You don't like oysters, Mr. Walraven?" Ivy asked politely.

"I'm sure they're quite good, but I don't do well with shellfish."

Will glanced down the table at his brother and raised his eyebrows at this understatement. The poor man had broken out in hives all over his face and stomach the first time he had lobster as a teenager. The doctor had advised him to avoid shellfish altogether.

Miss Lippincott, seated across the table, tilted her head. "How horrible for you, Mr. Walraven. I adore caviar and had the most wonderful lobster at the Casino dance last week." Her voice lowered. "Mrs. Astor and Mrs. Vanderbilt were in attendance. Much to my disappointment, they didn't argue, just ignored each other." Without pausing for breath, she continued, "Gertrude wore a lovely gown of pale blue moiré. She and I visit the same modiste in Paris."

Miss Lippincott sipped her wine and leveled a stare at Ivy. "Are you acquainted with Gertrude Vanderbilt, Miss King?"

The silly woman knew full well that daughters of bookshop owners didn't attend the same functions as New York society's Four Hundred.

Will started to speak in Ivy's defense, but she placed a hand on his arm. "I've not had the pleasure. I met her father, however, when I helped deliver supplies to the poor last winter. Mr. Vanderbilt sits on the Tribune Coal and Food Fund board." She refused to cower under this girl's scrutiny. "Have you ever served the needy, Miss Lippincott?"

An answer was not forthcoming. Instead, Miss Lippincott lifted her chin and turned to the young man beside her. "Tell me about the yacht race last weekend."

Good. Let the young man entertain the snobby woman.

Will bent close and whispered, "Bravo, Miss King."

A pretty blush rose in her cheeks. "I'm sorry. That was rude of me."

"Not at all. She had it coming."

The next three courses were served with much fanfare, and toward the end of the long meal, the footmen placed a mousse à l'orange in front of each guest. Will thought it cute the way Ivy's eyes widened at the decadent dessert.

"I'm going to need to go for a long bike ride to recover from this," she mumbled.

"Where do you like to ride?"

"My favorite spot is Central Park."

"Although I've had the pleasure of touring the Park, Will here's never been," Bert interjected. "Maybe you should both go. The fresh air would do him some good."

Mrs. Capp, who must have canine-like hearing, spoke before Miss King had the chance. "Splendid idea, Mr. Walraven. I refuse to ride in this heat, but Ivy's made of sterner stuff. I'm sure she'd like some company."

Will eased back in his chair and glared at his meddling brother behind Miss King's back.

Bert ignored Will's discomfort. "I understand there are several nice places to eat lunch there."

Miss King fiddled with the napkin in her lap. "I don't know. It's difficult to leave the shop for long on a Saturday. My grandmother tends to get overwhelmed."

"I'll help her," Mrs. Capp offered. "I've pitched in a time or two, so I'm not completely inept at selling a book." She winked at Bert. "And yes, the Casino is an excellent place to stop for a bite to eat."

Resigned or happy, he wasn't sure which, Will turned to his right. "Well, Miss King, what do you think? Would you mind giving me a tour of your famous park?"

She hesitated for a few embarrassing seconds, then gave a quick nod. "I'd be glad to. We can meet at Union Park Square. There's a shop near your hotel where you can rent a cycle for the day, if I'm not mistaken."

"I've seen it. What time shall I meet you?"

He wasn't sure he liked the way Miss King's lips twitched.

"Seven o'clock. I like to get to the park early, before the crowds."

"At that time, you'll get there before the birds," Will muttered.

Miss King covered her mouth with her hand, but not before Will caught her laugh.

"It will just be a leisurely drive around the park."

Why did he suspect that nothing Ivy did could be called leisurely?

FOURTEEN

Creeping out of her bedroom to avoid waking Gran, Ivy tiptoed past the kitchen. She usually skipped breakfast before work, preferring the extra sleep, and didn't want to disturb her grandmother by clanking dishes. Just as she reached the stairs, the floorboards behind her creaked.

Gran shuffled out of the kitchen. "I've made you something to eat to take with you," she said, handing Ivy an old lunch pail from her school days.

Ivy peeked inside and found a piece of Gran's fruitcake, a slice of cheese, a bottle of milk, and a napkin. Her heart swelled, and a lump formed in her throat. Gran couldn't replace Mama, but she was the best grandmother the Lord could have blessed her with. "Thanks, Gran."

Ivy's walk to work seemed lighter. The birds sang cheerfully, and people greeted her with friendly "Good mornings." The evening at the theatre and dinner with the Dixons the night before had been one of the best of her life. And she had a bike ride in Central Park to look forward to.

She hadn't had the chance to tell Gran about her planned outing, but Ivy doubted she'd object. If anything, she'd encourage her granddaughter to stay out all day with the handsome William Walraven.

Although Ivy would like nothing better, it wasn't fair to Gran or Zella to be gone for more than the morning. Furthermore, Saturdays were their busiest day, and she needed to make sure that everything was in order—the shop cleaned, and new books shelved —before she laid her head on her pillow. Ivy refused to leave those duties for her arthritic grandmother.

As always, her walk to work gave her mind an opportunity to wander, and not always where she wanted it to. This morning, she could think of nothing but tomorrow's ride in Central Park with William. Would he be embarrassed by her? She didn't own the latest cycling outfit. The wealthy who visited the park—who all knew each other and met in lively social circles—wouldn't know her from Adam. But they might know William.

And then there was her limp. Although it didn't affect her cycling, her platform boot stood out under her shorter-length riding skirt.

Maybe she should have thought this through before going along with Zella's matchmaking machinations.

Please, Lord, grant me one day of happiness. One day in which I don't feel different or unworthy.

Outside the library, the other librarians gathered on the steps until Mr. Collins arrived and opened the door. Remembering her conversation with Robert the night before, Ivy headed straight to the rare books room. Her stomach knotted at the thought of what she might find and what she might have to do about it.

She scanned the shelves, her eyes falling on the spot where the three Defoe volumes should be. They were gone. Her mind raced through the possibilities for why they were missing.

Not ready to declare them stolen, Ivy checked the desk where books waiting to be reshelved were placed. She sifted through the short pile, coming up empty-handed. With one more possibility in mind, she asked the other floor librarians if they'd seen the set, but no one had. A security guard patrolled the area during open hours, making periodic stops. But the room wasn't always manned, providing ample opportunity for an ambitious thief to slip out with a book.

Worry gnawed at her as she returned to her desk, her thoughts drifting to Jack McGill. She'd helped him several times in the rare books room, watching him examine various first editions with what seemed like genuine scholarly interest. But the thought of accusing a patron—even indirectly—made her stomach ache. What if she was wrong? What if there was an innocent explanation?

Her mother had always taught her that bearing false witness was one of the gravest sins, and the thought of potentially ruining someone's reputation made her feel ill. But if she stayed silent and Mr. McGill was responsible, how many other precious volumes might disappear from the library's collection?

When the head librarian arrived at eight thirty, Ivy knocked on his office door, still uncertain about how much to say. His deep voice boomed, "Come in, come in."

Ivy entered and approached his desk, her heart pounding.

Mr. Landing stood and motioned her to the chair before his desk. "Good morning, Miss King. Have a seat." He returned to his oversized leather chair and steepled his fingers. "How can I help you?"

"I'm sorry to bother you, but I can't find the three volumes of Defoe's *Robinson Crusoe*. The first edition set. I've looked everywhere and asked the other librarians, but no one has seen them. Do you know where they might be?"

His brow creased in thought. "Why, no, I don't. The last time I saw the books, they were all where they should be." He stood and walked around to the door of his office. "Let's go take a look, shall we?"

In the rare books room, Mr. Landing ran his hand along the spines of the books where the set was normally kept. He frowned and scratched his head. "Maybe they've been mis-shelved. Why were you looking for them?"

"An acquaintance described a set he'd just purchased, and it sounded like the Astor's copies." The words felt like rocks in her mouth, heavy with implication.

"Do you know where this acquaintance purchased his volumes?"

"He said it was from a man outside a bookshop near Holland House, where he's staying." Ivy wrestled with whether to mention her suspicions about Jack McGill but held back.

"I wish people would learn not to buy from people selling on the streets." Mr. Landing sighed heavily, and his shoulders drooped. "Can he bring the books in? I'd like to speak with him before contacting the police. If the books are indeed from the Astor collection, he must return them."

"I'm sure he'd be glad to come in." The relief of having shared the problem without naming names washed over her. Let the truth come out through proper channels. If Mr. McGill was involved, Robert's description of the seller would reveal that soon enough.

"Good," Mr. Landing said. "I'll speak with Mr. Collins to see if he knows anything and then have my secretary send your friend a message to come in. We will need to contact the police. Not that it will do any good." Mr. Landing walked to the nearest librarian's desk and picked up a notepad and pen. "Please write his name. And keep this hushed for now."

Ivy understood the need for discretion. If news got out that rare books were being pilfered from the Astor, donors might be more hesitant to gift their valuable collections. More than that, false accusations could destroy both reputations and careers.

She wrote down Robert's name and returned to her station, her mind whirling. Because of the time she'd spent with Mr. Landing, she was behind in the work she needed to finish before she could leave.

Moving about the floor quickly, she returned books to the

correct shelves and tidied the tables left in disarray by thoughtless visitors. Her hip ached, and at this rate, she wouldn't have the energy to finish her work at the shop by nightfall. The afternoon stretched before her like a mountain to climb. Two of her would be good right now.

But get it done she would, because tomorrow promised to be the best day of her life.

FIFTEEN

At seven sharp, Ivy wheeled her cycle to the base of the bronze statue of Lafayette in Union Square. William stood on the path behind the statue, bicycle at his side. She narrowly stopped a sigh from escaping her lips.

His fawn-colored tweed suit made his eyes appear more yellow than brown, reminding her of the druggist's tabby. Matching knickerbockers fit snugly around his hips and then fell in a straight line to his knees, where they tucked in squarely. His full lips quirked at her perusal.

"Good morning, Mr. Walraven. You found yourself a nice bicycle, I see. Good choice."

William yawned. "I have two requests."

"So soon?"

"They're important."

"Go on."

Will held up a finger, a mischievous gleam in his eyes. "First, call me Will. Otherwise, I'll keep glancing around for my father, who never calls me by my nickname." Another finger went up. "Second, I desperately need a cup of coffee before we hit the park."

He followed the declaration with a playful pout so disarming it could charm even the sternest of women.

Ivy bit her lip to keep from giggling like a schoolgirl. What was it about this man that made her want to turn her back on her responsibilities for the sheer enjoyment of life?

"I think we can arrange that..." She hesitated before trying his name on her lips for the first time. "Will. And you'd better call me Ivy."

With a gentle push of her foot, the bicycle surged forward. Her hands rested lightly on the handlebars and, as the wheels hummed beneath her, she swayed in time with the rhythm of the bicycle.

They rode up a less busy street, side by side. William leaned into the turns, handling the change in path like an expert.

"You're much better at this than you let on," Ivy called above the breeze.

"Well, it's been a while, but it's all coming back to me now."

William's smile was contagious, and Ivy grinned back.

A hint of peach tinged the scattered clouds, and the city's silhouette gradually emerged from the shadows.

They began their ride on the park's west side, passing rows of ornate brownstones with wide front entrances. However, as they rode farther into the park, it was as though they were leaving the city behind. Trees and grass dotted the landscape. At one point, they passed a shaggy dog herding a bunch of sheep.

Ivy laughed at Will's open mouth expression. "No, you're not seeing things. That's sheep all right."

Farther down the path, they pulled over to let a group of men on horseback pass.

"I believe you told me you ride." Ivy tilted her head toward the horses.

"I do, but not as much as I'd like."

As they approached a stone lookout tower on a hill, Ivy pointed. "That's the Belvedere. It's the highest point in the park and offers a wonderful view." Slowing to a stop, she hopped off her

bicycle and propped it against a lamppost. She'd love to challenge
him to a race to the top, but she knew her limitations. The last
thing she wanted was to appear foolish.

William set his bike next to hers. "Do you want to go up?" he
asked, tipping his head toward the tower. He seemed hesitant to
ask, probably because he was afraid she wouldn't make it and he'd
have to carry her.

But hours of bike riding and taking care of the bookshop had
made Ivy strong. Not fast, but she had endurance.

Steep stairs marched up the stone structure that resembled a
medieval castle, and they laughed gaily when they reached the top.

Will leaned against the wall and released a dramatic breath. "I
can't keep up with you."

He was joking, obviously, but a surge of pride shot through
her, and she thanked the Lord that her leg hadn't buckled on the
way up.

Ivy placed her hands on the wall and sighed at the enchanting
panorama before them. The park spread out below with its
smooth green lawns, shady groves, lakes, wooded dells, and vine-
covered arbors. Boats docked at various landings, waiting to be
enjoyed by countless visitors. She waved to a group of children
flying a kite.

"Did you fly kites as a child?" Will propped his forearms on the
top of the wall. He stood close, and the length of his body brushed
hers.

She tried to concentrate on his question. "Some. My mother
and father tried to get me out of the city as often as possible." The
memories of Sunday outings were ones she'd not thought of in a
long time.

How she missed her parents—their unconditional love and
steady presence in her life.

She glanced at the handsome man beside her, who made her
palms sweat and her heart flutter like a bird's wings.

What would Mama and Papa think of him? They'd never

taken to Ivy's former beau, especially Papa, who'd said he lacked strength of character. She'd ignored the warning, assuming her protective father wouldn't like any man Ivy brought home.

Still, Papa would like Will, she was certain.

"Come on, we've still lots to see." Ivy slid her hand into his and tugged him toward the stairs. When had she become so brazen?

Ivy pulled Will toward the lookout tower stairs, and his breath lodged in his chest when she turned and grinned at him. She had the most radiant smile he'd ever seen, and joy swept through him —unlike anything he'd felt in a long time.

A jaunty hat sat atop her head, and the slim-fitting jacket showed off her curvy figure. He could imagine slipping his hands around her waist and pulling her in for a kiss.

Before his thoughts got the better of him, Will's gaze slid to Ivy's shortened skirt, designed to keep the fabric from catching on the pedals. Her right shoe, with its inch-high platform, was in full view, but he barely noticed it. He just prayed her leg didn't cause her too much pain.

By the wide grin and her twinkling eyes, he assumed it didn't.

They continued through the northeastern end of the park. Sunlight filtered through the leaves, creating a dappled pattern on the path. The crunch of their wheels over the uneven terrain and the quiet of the morning was hypnotic. The tension that had been building for weeks eased, and Will wished for the day to stay care-free for both of them.

Tomorrow would be soon enough to tell her who he really was.

He prayed she'd still want his company.

The gentle breeze carried the earthy aroma of soil and water. Soon, a large lake came into view, its glassy surface reflecting the azure sky and verdant hues of the park. Willow trees lined the water's edge, their graceful branches trailing in the water, while Egyptian lotus dotted the lake's surface.

They coasted along the shore, cool shadows alternating with the sun's warmth as they wheeled along. Ivy pointed to a collection of hills and bluffs. "Over that way is McGowan's Pass. In the American Revolution, George Washington led his troops through here in the fall of 1776. McGowan's Pass Tavern is nestled in those hills and is known to have a few rabble-rousers as patrons."

They rounded the hill past the historic building, and Will picked up speed. Ivy shouted to slow down, but he was already moving at a good clip, thoroughly enjoying himself. He put his feet on the footrests and coasted down the hill, passing a park policeman who waved. Will waved back.

Soon, he realized the policeman was sprinting after him, and on the breeze, Will thought he caught the word *halt*. Will slowed to a gradual stop, uncertain.

His face ruddy and chest heaving, the policeman marched to Will's bike. Ivy rolled up behind him.

"Do you know there's a law against scorching?" the officer demanded.

Will removed his cap and ran a hand through his sweat-damp hair. "Scorching?"

"You can't go over twelve miles per hour," Ivy said. She turned to the officer and glanced at his badge. "Officer Murphy, it's my fault. My friend here is from Philadelphia," she rolled her eyes as though that information spoke volumes, "and I was remiss in explaining our cycling laws."

"I should book you into the substation."

Ivy set her bike on the ground and approached the officer. She smiled warmly and laid a hand on his arm. "Please, Captain Murphy."

"That's Sergeant Murphy." He puffed himself up.

"Oh, I thought for sure..." Her eyelashes batted coquettishly.

Will nearly forgot how to breathe. Who knew this lovely woman could be such a flirt? Could he get her to do the same with him?

She clasped her hands and placed them over her heart. "Please, sir, have mercy on my unwitting friend. I promise it won't happen again."

The sergeant cleared his throat, visibly unsettled. Will couldn't blame him—anyone might falter under the gaze of wide eyes as blue as a cloudless summer sky.

"Yes, well, I can't let him off scot-free," Sergeant Murphy said as he pulled out a pad of paper from a pocket inside his coat. "Name?"

"William Walraven."

Sergeant Murphy scribbled, ripped off a sheet from the pad, and handed it to Will. "It's a warning. But your name will now be in our records." He pointed a stubby finger at Will's chest. "Don't cause any more trouble." He strode off, probably looking for the next unsuspecting wheelman.

Will turned to Ivy, who burst out laughing.

"I'm glad you find this amusing. How did he know I was going over twelve miles per hour?"

"He guessed. But seriously, bikers mowing over pedestrians has become a hot topic in Manhattan, so the police have been understandably heavy-handed with issuing tickets. Lucky for you, I got you out of jail time."

Ivy lifted her bicycle off the ground and wheeled it toward the grass, where she leaned it against a tree. "Even though I think you'd look wonderful in prison garb." She grinned and ducked under a branch.

Will laughed and tugged at her jacket sleeve. He wasn't sure why, but he felt suddenly playful. She deftly moved away but tripped over a protruding root and fell onto the grass.

Startled, Will sank to his knees beside her. The dampness of the grass seeped through his pants. "Ivy? Blast it! Are you all right?" Her shoulders were shaking.

He ran a hand lightly over her back. "Let me help you. Tell me where it hurts." Panic clawed at his throat. "I'm an idiot. I'm so sorry."

She rolled over and peered up at him. "For what?" she giggled. "That's the most I've laughed in two years."

Relief flooded through him, and he collapsed on the ground next to her. When his racing heart returned to its normal rhythm, he couldn't help but laugh along with her.

When their mirth finally subsided, she gazed at the sky and sighed. "Imagine flying like a bird—up above, all the difficulties of the earth below. It's so perfect up there, like something in a dream."

He turned his head and took in her profile. "Do you wish you could fly away? Is that what you dream of?" He wouldn't blame her if she did.

"No," she said quietly. "My desires are more grounded."

"I'd like to hear them." It was the truth. Getting to know her had become all important.

"It's silly, really, but I'd love to buy and sell rare books like we did when my parents were alive. I never got to go on any of their trips, but my mother used to tell me how exhilarating the hunt for a perfect book could be." Her voice trailed off, and she sighed.

Her wish seemed so simple, one that wouldn't give someone of his means a second thought about going after. Yet, the wistfulness in her voice told him she thought her dream was as unattainable as being able to soar like a bird.

The sudden urge to help her make it a reality stole his breath.

Ivy turned her head, and the grass tickled her nose as she stared at her companion. A soft smile lingered on his face, their laughter fading into an electric anticipation. Just a few inches separated their lips.

He gently plucked a piece of grass from her hair, his hand grazing her face as it slid away.

Part of her wanted to be kissed. But doubt as to where this tentative relationship would lead crept in. She pushed herself to a sitting position and placed her hat back on her head. "Up ahead is The Metropolitan Museum of Art and the Obelisk. What time is it?"

Will looked at the leather-strapped watch on his wrist. "It's after ten." He stood and held a hand out to help her up.

"Then it should be open."

When they reached their bicycles, he held her handlebar while she swung her leg over the cycle.

"Thank you," she said, looking up into his face.

"You're most welcome." His eyes roamed over her face as if searching for something. "In case I don't say it later, this is the most enjoyable day I've had in a long time."

"Me too." Her voice came out in a whisper.

They made their way around the east end of the Park reservoir and up the driveway to the museum, passing the famous monument given to the city by the Khedive of Egypt. Once they parked and locked their bicycles, they strolled to the museum, her arm through his.

Inside the quiet building, they perused halls of modern sculptures, ancient terracotta, musical instruments from around the world, tapestries, and famous paintings.

Ivy shuddered at the Egyptian mummies, and Will laughed, slinging an arm around her shoulders.

"Don't worry, I'll protect you."

The warmth of his arm around her made her heart sing.

Even though the gesture was fleeting, the sensation lingered.

Despite telling herself a thousand times that she didn't need a man, Ivy couldn't deny the wonderful feeling of being cared for.

She slipped her hand through his arm, and they continued their trek through the museum. They wandered around glass displays of elegant jewelry and lace, some donated by the Astor family and made of exquisite tracery.

In one hall hung Makart's colossal painting of Diana and her hunting party. The piece was so large it was almost lifelike. Stunning in detail, the figures depicted were all women in various stages of dress. Ivy's cheeks warmed when Will stopped beside her to view the painting.

"I don't remember ever attending a hunt like that," he said cheekily.

Ivy nudged him and smiled. "That's good to know. I'd have been worried otherwise."

They left the museum an hour later. The park had filled up since they'd been inside. Riding clubs in parades of satin-coated horses trotted along the drives. The city's fashionable crowd emerged in their private barouches and coupes along the park's main driveway. A Sousa band warmed up at a bandstand. Clad in embroidered black-on-black with lots of gold trim and braid, the group played everything from orchestral to patriotic music.

"Would you like to see the menagerie?" Ivy asked. "It's the last site on my tour."

"Let's go, then. Far be it for me to say I didn't follow my guide's suggestions."

They wandered through the castellated gray brick building covered in clinging vines, visiting cages of exotic birds, elephants, polar bears, bison, hippopotami, and sea lions. At one cage, a gorgeous leopard paced back and forth on its small enclosure's packed dirt floor.

"Although we're fortunate to see animals we might never get a chance to see otherwise, I wish they didn't have to be locked up." Ivy felt a strange kinship with the poor animal. She turned away from the cage, not wanting to dwell on the depressing sight any longer.

At the monkey cages, a pair of little boys tried to capture the attention of the inhabitants. Their antics, including scratching their heads like they had fleas, had Ivy laughing until her sides ached.

"Bert and I used to do that when we visited the Philadelphia Zoo. Our governess would always get so embarrassed."

A governess? There was so much about William Walraven she didn't know. He could probably afford things she'd never dreamed of and knew many people in his social circle who had similar backgrounds. What was he doing with a woman like her?

"Are you hungry?" he asked as they exited the menagerie. "We could get some lunch."

As much as Ivy wanted to spend more time with him, she also questioned her sanity. She could easily lose her head over this man. "Thank you, but no. I should head home. Although I know Zella will do her best to help Gran, I can't be away the entire day."

"Would you mind if Bert and I joined you for church tomorrow?" Will asked as they stopped just outside the park's south entrance. His voice was tentative, as if he expected her to say no.

How could she refuse? "I'm sure Gran would love that. We'll see you at ten." She placed her leg over the bicycle frame and started to push away. She glanced back one last time to find him grinning from ear to ear.

Sixteen

Ivy stepped out of her bedroom, dressed for church and in a grand mood. The Central Park outing had been the most wonderful of her life. Will made for excellent company, and experiencing the park through the eyes of a visitor made her appreciate it more than ever.

Her only regret was that she hadn't let her inhibitions go long enough for him to kiss her.

Gran was already bustling about, setting the kettle on the stove as Ivy entered the kitchen for coffee.

"Good morning, dear," Gran said, glancing up. "How did you sleep?"

"Like a log."

"All that fresh air, I suspect."

"Don't forget, the Walravens are coming to church with us."

"I haven't forgotten." Gran sliced a loaf of bread and laid the pieces on a plate. "The newspaper is on the table. I haven't read it yet, but you go ahead. I'll look at it later."

Ivy pulled a cup from the cupboard, poured some coffee, and slid into a chair by the window.

"I need to check on something in the shop," Gran called out, already heading for the stairs. "Finish your breakfast, dear."

"Thanks, Gran."

Ivy sipped her hot drink while her eyes scanned the headlines. The news of the day included another attempt to overthrow the Spanish monarchy and worries over the impact on Cuba. England reported a new commander-in-chief of its army. The Brooklyn Bridegrooms had soundly defeated the Giants seven to two.

And a department store was moving into the old Heinrich's dry goods building.

So, the rumors had been correct.

She plunked down her cup and sat up straighter in her chair, placing the paper on the table in front of her. The journalist reported that the dry goods store had been purchased by a group out of Philadelphia who already owned department stores in Philadelphia, Pittsburgh, and Chicago.

Her heart thudded as the name of the store's general manager screamed from the page—William Walraven, son of department store mogul Charles Walraven.

Ivy stared at the words until they blurred, her mind racing back through every moment with Will. Her chest tightened as she remembered daydreaming just that morning about a future with him. She'd even gone so far as to let her mind wander to children with hazel eyes and cleft chins who loved literature and bicycling.

Sensing her distress, Dickens padded over and laid his massive head on her lap. She absently scratched behind his ears, finding comfort in his warm presence.

"Oh, Dickens," she whispered, her voice trembling. "I've been such a fool. Yesterday in the park, I thought..." She trailed off, remembering how Will had looked at her as they strolled through the museum, how his hand had brushed against hers more than once. How they almost kissed. "I thought he might actually care for me. But he doesn't even respect me enough to tell me the truth."

She stood abruptly, causing Dickens to lift his head. Moving to the cupboard, she pulled out his breakfast, the routine helping to steady her shaking hands. He barked when she stopped and stared at the empty dog bowl before her. "At least you're honest about what you want," she told the dog as she filled his bowl.

Returning to the paper, Ivy read the article again, each word striking like a physical blow. A department store. Not just any department store, but a giant from Philadelphia, reaching its tentacles into her beloved neighborhood. And Will—charming, intelligent Will—was not only there to see the store up and running, but was also the son of the family that owned the company.

She swiped a hand down her face, thinking of how foolish she was when she'd imagined he came from a family with enough money to afford a governess and a few servants. No, it would seem this family owned a large chunk of Philadelphia real estate.

Her face burned with humiliation as she realized how easily she'd been deceived. Had he laughed about it later with Bert, about how the naïve bookseller's daughter never guessed who they were?

She glanced at the clock. The Walravens should be at the shop any minute. Ivy's anger crystallized into something hard and sharp in her chest. She stood, smoothing her church dress with trembling hands, drawing herself up to her full height.

They would not find her crying. They would not find her broken. They would find her fury.

⊹⊹⊷⊷⊹⊹

Instead of reading the Sunday newspaper first thing or poring over reports on the status of the Denwall project, Will had spent a leisurely morning with a book he'd borrowed from Bert.

Nothing wrong with taking an interest in something so important to Ivy.

What caught him off guard was that he actually enjoyed the

work of fiction, and the pleasant morning had flown by. No headache slipped in behind his eyes. No worry cramped his stomach. Instead, Will looked forward to spending the rest of the day with the woman who'd stolen his heart while on a bicycle ride through Central Park.

By five minutes to ten, he and Bert had arrived at the bookshop to escort Ivy and her grandmother to church. Bert rang the doorbell and soon Mrs. King appeared, waving them inside.

"Come in, come in," she said as she opened the door. "It's so good of you to join us this morning. Ivy will be right down."

Will took off his hat and ran a hand through his hair, glancing around the shop.

"I understand you had a grand time yesterday," Mrs. King remarked.

Will looked toward the back room door. "Yes, it was a nice day. Miss King is a terrific tour guide."

Mrs. King adjusted her shawl around her shoulders. "Having lived here all her life, Ivy knows the city well. And she's such a smart young woman. She'd make any man an excellent wife." Her eyes sparkled with enthusiasm.

Bert grinned and nudged Will with his elbow.

Will refused to comment, not wanting to incriminate himself.

Mrs. King eyed the back room door. "I don't know what could be keeping Ivy. Let me just run up and tell her you're here."

A few minutes later, raised voices and a thump in the apartment above made Will lift his eyebrows in concern. Was everything all right up there?

Ivy burst through the back door, clutching a newspaper in her hand. Her grandmother trailed behind, her mouth pinched.

"Good morning, Ivy." Will tipped his hat.

"That's *Miss King* to you, Mr. Walraven." Ivy said, her eyes glaring, and her cheeks flushed with anger.

"Is everything all right?" He suspected it wasn't.

Ivy marched toward him, waving the newspaper in front of his face. "Why didn't you tell me?"

Dread crept through Will's veins. "Tell you what?"

"That *you* are the Walravens of Denwall Department Stores. And you're opening an emporium not two blocks from here."

So, Sage had released his article a full week early. A heads-up would have been nice.

Pride in his family's business had Will squaring his shoulders. "Yes, it's our fifth store. Is that a problem?"

"Of course it's a problem. We met at an anti-department store rally, for goodness' sake." Ivy marched over to the counter, pulled out the pamphlet Will had seen a few weeks ago, and slammed it down. Her cheeks flared with color, and her eyes were as cold as a winter morning.

He'd never seen her quite like this—strong-willed, yes, but not this fiery. And though she looked almost unshakable, he sensed a thread of vulnerability beneath her anger, something that made him feel both guilty and captivated. The pamphlet lay between them, its corners bent from her grip, a reminder of the gulf between his world and hers.

Ivy crossed her arms over her chest, her chin lifted, and her fingers tightened into determined fists as if she were restraining herself from punching him in the face.

Will tried to control his mounting frustration. "Have you stopped to think that a department store could actually help your business?"

Ivy snorted. "Really? How so?"

"We'll bring customers to this area who might not normally come this way to shop." His hand gestured toward the window. "They'll pass by your store, and if you have a fetching display, they might stop in. Purchase something, even. That's an opportunity you didn't have before."

Ivy wagged a finger at him. "I've heard of the practices you emporiums—you, you vultures—take part in. You have the money to influence the men in office to pass ordinances that benefit you and hurt the small shop owner."

"Buy favor, you mean?" Will kept his voice even, but his tone grew hard. "Denwall doesn't use bribery to get ahead, Miss King."

"Then what was that building commissioner doing at the theatre the other night?"

"I didn't invite him."

"Maybe not, but you knew he was coming," Ivy said. "I'm assuming George Dixon made a trade of some sort with you. Give *The Daily New Yorker* the first interview, and he'd bring you the building commission on a platter."

"I won't pass up a chance to get ahead of rumors. So I gave Dixon's newspaper an interview with no preconceived notion of a quid pro quo. It was Dixon's decision alone to invite a member of the building commission."

Will struggled to keep his voice steady. "I took advantage of the get-together to convince him that the commission was unnecessarily holding up Denwall's progress. But I didn't influence the commissioner by bribing him." His father may have been controlling when it came to Denwall and his family, but he'd never offered a bribe to anyone. And neither would Will.

Ivy stepped back, the air crackling with tension. "Tell me this. Are you, or are you not, going to sell books in your store?"

Will pinched the bridge of his nose as a headache formed behind his brow. "Yes, we plan to have a department devoted to books and stationery."

"And you don't think that's going to cause us problems? I know full well you can sell cheaper than we can."

"That's a valid point. However, if you do your job right," Will pointed his finger at her, "you'll bring customers in with your personalized and charming service. We can't compete with that." Will wasn't sure what else he could say. The day that had started with joyful anticipation had turned into a disaster.

"I guess we'll have to see, won't we?" Ivy threw down the proverbial gauntlet.

"I guess so."

"But if you weren't worried about the ramifications of moving into this neighborhood and what I might think, why did you lie to me?"

Will stepped back and shoved his hands in his pockets. "I never lied to you."

"You didn't tell me what your business in New York entailed."

"You never asked. If you had, I would have answered truthfully." Such a childish, flimsy excuse.

She scoffed. "I'll grant that you may not have lied outright, but you purposefully hid the truth. It was a lie of omission."

Will shrugged in defeat. "I wasn't even sure I'd ever see you again, when you gave me the cold shoulder after church. And yesterday, we were having so much fun, I didn't want to spoil it. I planned to tell you today."

"Speaking of church, we're going to be late." Mrs. King's cheery voice sounded forced as she wrung her hands, her eyes darting between Ivy and Will.

"I'm not going to church this morning, Gran. I'll attend the evening services instead." Ivy pulled back her shoulders and marched to the back room. She opened the door and slammed it behind her.

SEVENTEEN

Will sat in his makeshift office on the top floor of Denwall and ran his fingers through his already disheveled hair. The morning light streaming through the window seemed harsh and unforgiving, much like his current circumstances.

His thoughts constantly drifted to Ivy's face—the way her eyes had flashed with betrayal, the tight set of her jaw as she'd dismissed him. A hollowness resided in his chest since the disastrous incident at the bookshop.

Will tried to convince himself to let go of her. She wasn't right for him anyway—though that hardly mattered now, given how much she clearly loathed him. At times, he managed to justify his actions, reminding himself he'd never lied. Furthermore, he'd intended to tell her about his family's business but had lost the battle with time.

He pushed his palms into his eyes. *Focus. You have more pressing issues to deal with.*

Like preparing for Denwall's grand opening.

He stared at the latest correspondence from his father. Charles Walraven's neat, precise handwriting filled page after page with questions about progress, demands for faster results, and thinly veiled disappointment. The last lines were particularly cutting:

I expected better from you, William. Perhaps I was hasty in thinking you ready for such responsibility.

The weight of the Walraven name had never felt heavier. Here he was, trying to prove himself worthy of his inheritance, and instead, he'd managed to alienate the one person—the one woman —who'd made him feel like more than just his father's son.

A knock preceded Bert's entrance. "The first employee interviews are in an hour. I thought we'd go over a few things first." He sat in the chair in front of Will's desk and propped up his feet.

"I've been working up the numbers for the change in the display window specifications the architect suggested. It will cost us time and money, but I think he's correct. The bigger windows will be more attractive."

Will suppressed a groan. "So many delays." The setbacks at the beginning of the project had already left them scrambling to stay on schedule. Avoidable mistakes might be made if they rushed, causing even more delays. "Do you think we need to hire even more men?"

"Owens has the men working overtime to get us back on schedule," Bert said.

"I don't think it's enough. How long will it take you to work up cost projections accounting for more manpower? Maybe give us two or three scenarios to compare."

"I can have figures ready this evening. I'll start as soon as the interviews are over."

"Sounds good." Will prayed they'd be able to hire at least ten more men for Owens's crew.

Bert slid a note across Will's desk. "This came by messenger earlier."

"What is it?"

"A message from Dixon. He says there's to be a neighborhood meeting this evening—a smoker—regarding Denwall. It's at

Hardman Hall on Nineteenth Street and Fifth Avenue. Not too far from here. Dixon suggests we attend to give our side of the story."

Will read the note and sighed. Being in charge wasn't all wining and dining the powerful men of the city. "I agree with him. We should go. A one-sided meeting will worsen matters. The local businessmen will get themselves all worked up over the unknown. If we're there to answer questions, it might put them at ease and make it easier for Denwall in the long run."

Bert shoved his glasses up his nose. "I hate public speaking," he grumbled.

"I can speak on behalf of Denwall, if you'd like."

Bert nodded. "Be my guest."

"I'll write up some notes before we go, so you can look them over." Will knew Denwall would be good for this community—he had the results to back up that belief—and he'd convince them of it.

Swinging his legs off the desk, Bert tapped a finger on the wood surface. "With that settled, let's talk about the interviews."

Will pulled his notepad from his top drawer. "Just so we're on the same page, we'll both interview the four men for the general manager's position. Then we'll split up and each take the applicants for department heads. Do you have a preference on which ones you'd like to take?"

"I wouldn't mind interviewing the stationary and the furnishing department applicants. Neither menswear nor womenswear are exactly my forte."

That was putting it mildly. "We need to impress upon each candidate that we don't have any time to waste. I want them all interviewing applicants for their departments starting next week."

Bert narrowed his eyes. "Do you think we can get all of this done and the store opened by the nineteenth?"

Will ran a hand around the back of his tense neck. "It will be tight."

"Have you looked at yourself in the mirror lately? You're a mess." His brother didn't bother sugarcoating his opinion.

Yes, he'd caught a glimpse of his reflection in the mirror that morning. His hair needed trimming. Dark circles loomed under his eyes, evidence of his sleepless nights. He looked worse than Bert on his most disheveled days.

"You've got to get over this obsession of pleasing Father, Will."

"You're saying you don't care?"

"I'm not saying that at all. But I don't let it run my life."

This was probably true. Bert walked the middle line between Will's need to impress their father and Ned's desire to thwart everything Father wanted of him.

Will exhaled, slumping back in his seat. "Old habits die hard, but you're right. I'd move the date of the opening back to where it was originally. Unfortunately, it's impossible at this point."

Bert cocked his head. "Is that the only thing bothering you?"

"I don't know what you're talking about." Will shuffled the papers on his desk.

"I'm assuming Denwall isn't the only problem keeping you up at night. You should tell her your sorry. Get down on your knees and beg her forgiveness."

Will didn't need to ask who Bert referred to. "Other than leaving town and taking Denwall with me, I doubt there's anything I can say that would persuade Miss King to forgive me."

"I don't know about that, but it's worth a try. She's good for you, you know."

Will didn't want to consider what he'd lost by deceiving Ivy. Too painful. Too energy draining. He glanced at his watch. "The first interview should be here any minute."

Bert stood, shaking his head all the way to the door. "I'll come back after we're done."

Several moments later their shared secretary ushered the first interviewee into the room. Will stood and forced all other thoughts from his mind except hiring the best employees.

By the end of the fourth interview, his head pounded. None of the men seemed right for the job as general manager of the store he'd spent the last two months building. He wanted only the best. Was he being too picky or critical?

After completing the interviews, Bert joined Will in the board office, kicking his feet up on the desk. "How did you do? I had some splendid candidates."

"I didn't think any of the applicants for general manager suited."

Bert studied Will's face. "I looked at their credentials. Unless they were all sporting horns and a tail, I can't believe there wasn't one good candidate."

"Call it gut instinct."

"Or you don't want to let go." Bert removed his spectacles and gave them a wipe with his handkerchief. "Like Father not wanting to let go of Denwall, even to you."

"My, my, but you are full of pearls of wisdom today." Will should tell his brother to mind his own business. Yet he knew Bert was right. Both about Ivy and about his growing attachment to New York. He'd enjoyed working on this project from the ground up. And truth be told, the hours he spent with the blue-eyed bookseller were the best of his life. The thought of returning to Philadelphia, of leaving things in shambles with Ivy, made his heart ache.

Eighteen

Will and Bert walked to the neighborhood meeting rather than arrive in the Denwall carriage. No point setting people's teeth on edge before the meeting was even called to order.

The packed hall was filled with small business owners who had come to voice their grievances. Men of all ages wore expressions varying from clenched jaws to resentful glares. Some were seated on wooden chairs dotting the room, while others stood in small clusters and engaged in heated conversations.

The gaslight fixtures hanging from the low ceiling cast a cold, flickering glow over the room. Will's eyes darted to the polished brass clock on the wall, its hands pointing to five minutes to seven.

Bert stopped beside Will just inside the doorway of the packed hall. "Why do I feel like Daniel entering the lion's den?"

"I'm not sure we'll be spared like Daniel. In retrospect, I should have prayed more fervently."

They stepped into the room, and a hush came over the place as the glances of the attendees turned their way. Will strode to the nearest group and introduced himself. Some returned his handshake, while others turned their backs before he reached them. All in all, the reception was much like he expected.

Will followed Bert to the front of the room where they took two vacant seats in the first row. A large man with a booming voice took the podium and introduced himself as Peter Jones, grocer. He stopped and glared when a commotion ensued at the back of the room.

Shifting in his seat, Will dug his fingers into his thigh at the sight of Ivy and her grandmother being blocked by two men at the door.

A fist thumped the podium. "Here, now, this is a businessman's meeting." The burly speaker emphasized the "man" in the nomenclature.

"I have every right to be here. As you know, Mr. Jones, my family owns a bookshop in this neighborhood." Ivy's voice carried to the front of the room.

Someone a few rows back called out, "Then one of your men should be here."

She lifted her chin and straightened her shoulders. "My father is deceased, and there are no other men in my family. My grandmother and I are here to represent our store. You can't keep us out."

A man beside Ivy grabbed her arm and started pulling her out the door. Will's fists balled of their own volition, and he stood. "Let her go."

His eyes locked onto hers, stormy blue and filled with trepidation. An unexpected surge of protectiveness tightened his chest. She was even more beautiful—and vulnerable—than he'd dared to remember.

Jones thumped the podium yet again. "Listen, here, Walraven. I don't know how you do things in Philadelphia, but our womenfolk stay home around here."

Mrs. King brushed by the man who'd had the good sense to let go of Ivy's arm. "You listen here, Peter Jones. I knew you when you were in nappies. Your mother would be ashamed of you."

Jones mumbled something unintelligible and turned beet red.

Will raised his voice above the din. "Mrs. King and Miss King are with me. Let them in."

Ivy opened her mouth, her blue eyes glacial in intensity, but her grandmother put her hand on her arm and pulled her to a bench.

Once the room quieted, Jones wiped his brow with a handkerchief and began again. "Gentlemen—and ladies—I believe you all know why we're here tonight. The thing we feared has happened. The department store is here. In our neighborhood. It's a challenge to our businesses, and we must discuss adapting to or fighting this new reality."

His gaze swept the room. "I'd like to give everyone here a chance to speak if they wish, but let's do this in an orderly manner. Raise your hand and, when called, please come up to the podium so everyone here can see you."

As the meeting progressed, various business owners shared their misgivings about Denwall. Some spoke of its economic threat, while others highlighted the potential benefits of increased foot traffic in the area. When it was Will's turn to speak, he stood and made his way to the podium. The room fell silent, all eyes on him. He took a deep breath, prepared to address the crowd, knowing his words could defuse the tension or ignite it further.

He gripped the edges of the podium, feeling the weight of the room's collective attention. "Good evening, everyone." He strove to keep his tone confident but respectful. "My name is William Walraven, and I'm here representing Denwall. I have heard your concerns about our store opening in this neighborhood, and I want to address them."

A murmur rippled through the crowd, but he pressed on. "Many of you worry that Denwall will drive small businesses out. But I want to assure you our intention is not to harm but to thrive together. Denwall will bring jobs, boost the local economy, and draw more customers to this area. We are committed to being good neighbors."

A man in the back raised his hand and stood up. "How can you say that when your prices will undercut ours? People will flock to your store, leaving us with no customers!"

"I understand your concern, and we are taking measures to ensure we don't unfairly undercut local businesses. We're offering partnerships and collaborations to feature local products in Denwall, giving your goods a larger audience."

"And what about our employees? Will you poach them with promises of better pay?"

A fair concern. Emporiums often took the best workers from smaller shops. "Our goal isn't to take your employees but to create more opportunities for everyone. We believe in fair wages and good working conditions, and we hope by raising the standard, all businesses will benefit."

Ivy glared at him, eyes flashing. He couldn't deny the attraction to a woman who knew her own mind. Guilt gnawed at him yet again, but he tamped it down.

"If your employees already receive a fair wage, there's no reason for them to defect," he said.

Disgruntled murmurs met his last statement with grudging agreement.

"What about the character of our neighborhood?" Jones eyed Will with skepticism. "Denwall is a big city store, not a community shop. How will you fit in here?"

"We plan to adapt Denwall to fit the community, not the other way around. We'll host community events, invest in local schools, and support neighborhood initiatives. Denwall wants to be a part of this community, not just a business."

The room was silent for a moment, and then Ivy stood up. "Mr. Walraven, if Denwall is sincere in its commitment, why not set up a community advisory board?" Her voice was clear and firm. "Include representatives from local businesses and residents to ensure Denwall's integration benefits all."

"An excellent idea, Miss King." He was grateful for the suggestion. "We would be more than willing to establish a community advisory board. This way, we can work together, address concerns as they arise, and ensure Denwall's presence is positive."

There was a mix of nods and skeptical glances, but the atmosphere had shifted. Although they'd never needed to establish such a group in any other city where Denwall had opened stores, the company's board would surely agree to this step.

As long as his father didn't erect any walls just to be ornery.

Jones cleared his throat. "All right, Walraven. We'll give this community advisory board a try. But understand, we're watching you closely. One wrong move, and we'll be back here, demanding answers."

"Understood, Mr. Jones. We'll do everything in our power to earn your trust."

As the meeting adjourned, Will found Ivy and Mrs. King by the door. "Thank you for your suggestion, Miss King. I believe it made a real difference tonight."

She lifted her chin. "I didn't do it for you."

Apparently, she still held a grudge.

Mrs. King pointed her finger at Will. "You better make sure you keep your promises."

⊹━━◦◦━━⊹

Ivy moved around the shop from one chore to the next, unable to relax. Her nerves jittered from the tense atmosphere at the meeting of neighborhood businesses, where they'd almost refused her admittance.

The nerve of some men. If Will hadn't insisted she and Gran be allowed to stay, they would have been kicked out.

Truth be told, the shock of seeing Will and Bert at the gathering still lingered. They displayed a certain amount of courage to attend despite the crowd's antagonism toward Denwall. And Will's willingness to listen to an advisory board went a long way toward calming the agitated men.

Still, Ivy couldn't forgive him for his subterfuge, no matter how attractive his commanding presence.

Deep in thought, she jumped when a knock sounded at the door.

Whoever was out there could see her through the shop window, so she couldn't hide.

She looked over her shoulder, surprised to find Robert Walraven.

Ivy marched across the room and flipped the lock, her anger simmering. Although she was particularly furious with Will, she also held some resentment toward his brother. Bert could have mentioned their connection to Denwall just as easily as Will. They both, however, kept that piece of information a secret.

Bert removed his hat and ran his hand around its brim, taking a small step toward her. "Miss King, may I speak to you for a moment?"

Her back stiffened. "What do you want, Mr. Walraven?"

"I've come to apologize."

"For what, exactly? For the lies you told? For your cagey brother?"

"I won't try to justify our actions by saying we didn't lie to you. We should have told you from the beginning who we were and why we were in New York."

Ivy folded her arms across her chest. "Yes, you should have."

He pushed his glasses up his nose. "All I can say is Will felt he had his reasons for not telling you. He'd planned to, but the article in the paper beat him to it."

"I don't like subterfuge, Mr. Walraven. Life is complicated enough without hidden agendas."

"You're absolutely correct. However, I believe he'd hoped that if you got to know him first, you'd be able to see past our family connections."

Her heart twisted at the words she'd longed to hear less than a day ago. "You say he cares, yet at the same time, he thinks so little of me that he assumed I would judge his character based on his family's business because it may hurt mine?"

"I wouldn't put it that way, no." Bert shuffled his feet.

"What's done is done." She waved a dismissive hand. "Besides, he's not here, is he? If *he* wanted to salvage our friendship, he'd be here, not you."

"Will can be stubborn."

"As can I." She headed for the door but remembered her findings at the library on Friday. Had it only been five days ago? "I assume you received a note from the Astor Library about your Defoes? That they're stolen?" A twinge of satisfaction surged in her belly when Bert's face turned red.

"I have a meeting with the assistant librarian tomorrow to return the books. I assume he'll want me to fill out a police report as soon as possible."

"Good." At least something worthwhile came out of her brief acquaintance with the conniving Walraven brothers. She pressed her lips together and marched to the door, flinging it open with gusto.

He sighed, placed his hat on his head, and moved toward the threshold. And yet, stopped short of leaving. He held out his hand, and she reluctantly took it. In a chivalrous move that surprised her, he lifted her hand and brushed a light kiss across the top. "Goodbye, Miss King. It has been a pleasure knowing you. I wish you all the best."

His hazel eyes—so much like Will's—searched her face once more before he turned and walked out the door.

Grief for what she'd lost sliced through her. She'd allowed the idea of a future with Will to seep into her dreams. Foolish, foolish woman. She knew better.

NINETEEN

The morning following the neighborhood meeting, Will paced the Holland House lobby and checked his watch for the third time since coming downstairs.

Where was Bert? He should have been back from his morning walk by now. They were supposed to meet Owens at the store in a few minutes to discuss the timetable. Hopefully, his brother would return to the hotel soon. Will left a note at the front desk in case Bert returned to the hotel before heading to the Denwall job site.

As he pushed open the door and entered the building, the sounds hit Will first—a chorus of rhythmic tapping and wood scraping against wood. Each blow of the hammer against a nail reverberated through the building. The air was thick with the earthy scent of freshly sawn timber mingled with sweat. A welcome sight—fifty or more men were hard at work, bringing the store to life.

He stepped closer, his boots clapping against the black and white tiled floor. The men glanced in his direction, acknowledging his arrival with a nod or a smile before returning to their tasks. Owens barked orders from the stairs to men on the second floor. When he saw Will, he grinned and walked to the main floor.

"What do you think, Mr. Walraven?" Owens asked.

"Looks like progress to me, Bob." Will shook the man's outstretched hand. "I don't suppose you've seen my brother by chance?"

"Not this morning."

It was almost nine o'clock. *Blast it all*. Bert may be the oldest, but sometimes Will felt like his keeper.

They strode down to the subbasement to check on the pneumatic tubing and back upstairs to inspect the work completed on each floor. Owens promised to give him a daily written report of accomplishments and tasks yet to be finished.

"I'm going back to the hotel to see what happened to Bert," he told Owens after they arrived at the main floor. "Just have your report delivered to the hotel this evening."

Will hailed a carriage and arrived at Holland House ten minutes later. The desk clerk he spoke to earlier was still on duty.

"Did my brother ever come back to the hotel?"

"No, sir, and I've been watching closely."

A knot of worry clenched at Will's stomach. As the sun reached its zenith in the sky, each passing minute amplified his unease. He looked around for any sign of his brother's familiar figure, the well-worn hat, or the easy stride that was recognizable even from a distance.

Had something gone wrong? Was there an accident? The rational part of him tried to dismiss these worries, to remind himself that delays were common, that there could be a logical explanation. Yet, the irrational whispers of anxiety persisted, growing louder each minute.

He headed out the door. The best place to start looking for Bert would be Madison Square Park, where he went every morning. Maybe he'd fallen asleep on a park bench.

Two city policemen brushed by him and entered the hotel. Will's muscles tensed, and he followed the officers to the front desk.

"Do you have a man staying here named Walraven?"

"I'm William Walraven," Will said from behind the men. "I'm staying here, as is my brother, Robert. Has something happened?" His throat tightened with each word.

"There was a mugging at the park a few hours ago. The victim has been taken to New York Hospital on Fifteenth Street." The policeman looked up from his notepad and retrieved a piece of paper from his jacket pocket. "He had a book with the name Walraven in it and a piece of hotel stationery inside."

Panic came fast and furious. "Is he all right?"

"He's badly hurt, sir. A bash on the head, and he appears to have taken some blows to his stomach and legs. He's not awoken."

Will turned to the hotel manager. "Will you have my carriage brought around immediately?"

"Already done, sir. And rest assured, New York Hospital is a fine institution. He'll be in good hands."

The shorter of the two policemen nodded. "Since he appeared to be a resident of Holland House, we assumed a private hospital might be in his best interest. It's not very far."

As the carriage rolled down Fifth Avenue, Will wanted to jump out and run to the hospital. Couldn't they move any faster? Up ahead, he could see the ornate brick and stone building that must be the place. Not wanting to wait any longer, he tapped on the roof and hopped down before the vehicle stopped.

The interior of the hospital appeared tidy and well-staffed. A nurse at the front desk summoned the house physician, and a dark-haired man in a rumpled white coat and loosened tie soon arrived.

"Your brother has a concussion from a nasty blow to the head. He also sustained injuries to his abdomen and legs, probably kicked. But those injuries aren't severe and will heal. No broken bones."

Will wanted to kill the person who'd done this to Bert, one of the gentlest souls he'd ever met. "He's not said anything?"

"No. Mr. Walraven has been unconscious since he arrived by ambulance about four hours ago."

"Is he going to be all right?" Will couldn't bear it if he wasn't.

The doctor's face didn't reflect discernible concern or optimism. "Only time will tell."

The close-to-the-vest demeanor of doctors wasn't new to Will. His father's doctor had been just as reticent to answer questions straightforwardly. "May I see him?"

"Certainly. I'll have Nurse Crump take you to the ward."

The ward occupied a spacious, well-lit room with tall windows adorned with heavy curtains drawn halfway to control the afternoon sunlight streaming in. The parquet floors shone from constant care. A nurse's station sat just inside the doorway, and a row of beds with crisp white sheets lined the back of the room between the window frames. The smell of antiseptic solution hit Will's nose.

"Your brother is over here." The nurse pointed to a bed in the far corner of the room.

Will swallowed the lump in his throat as he approached the bed. The taste of copper filled his mouth from biting the inside of his cheek to keep from yelling aloud at the sight of Bert—eyes closed, a white bandage swathed around his head. Dried blood matted his hair, and his breath came in short rasps as he inhaled and exhaled.

Guilt and fear churned in Will's stomach. Guilt for thinking the worst of Bert when he didn't show up at the job site. And fear that he might never hear his brother speak again. Or worse.

<hr>

Although there were many days Ivy stayed behind a few minutes to help a library patron or shelve one more book, today she needed to leave on time.

All morning, she'd been anxious about a large delivery the bookshop was expecting from its main supplier. Rumors had been circulating among booksellers of recent shipments arriving short or with damaged goods. Delivery men didn't tarry long for a shop owner to check their deliveries, and once they were out the door, the shipment was as good as received.

Not wanting to waste another minute, she spent the money to take the streetcar home. Entering the shop, she spotted Gran bent over boxes of deliveries, with a man tapping his foot next to her.

"Look, I've got deliveries to make. I can't wait all day, lady."

"Gran," Ivy called, "I'm parched. Would you mind putting the kettle on?"

Gran looked up and blinked several times. "Of course, dear."

When she left the room, Ivy slipped off her hat and gloves, placing them on the counter. She grabbed a pair of scissors from a drawer and pointed them at the delivery man. "You'll wait until I've had a chance to inspect the deliveries." Her tone was biting. "And if I ever hear you speak in that tone to my grandmother again, I'll report you to the publisher."

He stepped back, his hands out. "All right, miss. Have at it, but I leave in five minutes. I sincerely doubt a cripple such as yourself will go any faster than an old woman."

The cruel words knifed through Ivy, followed closely by anger and disappointment in her fellow man. Yes, she was crippled, but he had no right to call Gran an old woman. Had Ivy been a violent person, she would have thrown her scissors at the lug's head. Instead, she took a fortifying breath.

Twine snapped as it fell from around the top box.

The order form listing the goods shipped sat atop a stack of haphazardly packed books. She held the list with one hand and extracted each book with the other. At least three books were missing, and another five were damaged.

She marked up the bill of goods and waved it in front of the delivery man. "I need you to sign that you confirm some books are damaged and three are missing."

"I ain't signing nothing." The man folded his beefy arms over his chest.

"Then I don't accept this delivery. You can take these boxes back to the publisher and explain why they've lost a sale. Believe me, I will tell them personally what happened here."

"Fine." He signed the paper and stalked from the store.

Her threat to the delivery man had been all bravado. Publishers didn't care about a small business like the King bookshop. Their concern was more with the larger stores, such as the Charles Scribner's of the world.

Ivy sank into a nearby chair as her throat tightened. She hated to cry. It only led to a pounding headache. Pressing the heels of both hands to her eyes, she fought back the wave of threatening tears. Despite her efforts, wetness trickled down her cheeks.

Why, oh why, must everything in her life be an uphill battle? She'd not done anything to make God angry, had she? Her parents had been the salt of the earth, yet they'd been taken to Heaven much too soon.

She recalled the Bible verse her mother recited often when Ivy was a child and upset that she wasn't like other children. *For our light affliction, which is but for a moment, worketh for us a far more exceeding and eternal weight of glory.*

Ivy dabbed her eyes and blew her nose. Pocketing the handkerchief, she stood on shaky legs. In the bathroom, she washed her face and tucked some loose tendrils of hair behind her ear. Her pale face and swollen red eyes stared back at her in the beveled mirror.

What plan do you have for me, Lord? Are you using my trials for a greater good?

She straightened her shoulders. No more self-pity. She had a bookshop to run and a grandmother to take care of.

TWENTY

Ivy and Gran worked in silence for the rest of the afternoon. Several regular customers came into the store and made purchases and the shop even had a few new patrons who were very curious about the Denwall store. Thankfully, they all bought books from the King bookshop.

By the end of the day, Ivy was emotionally and physically spent. Generous to a fault, Zella bustled into the shop carrying a brown bag. Ivy shut the cash register drawer. "What do you have there?" The smoky aroma of pastrami, mixed with tangy sauerkraut, wafted in the air.

Dickens, who had been sound asleep on his blanket, sat up and thumped his tail.

"I've brought sandwiches for dinner. To give your grandmother a night off."

"That's thoughtful of you, Zell. Let me close the shop, and we'll go upstairs." The door jangled as Ivy bent down to lock their cash box. She huffed out a breath and lifted her head. On the other side of the counter stood a uniformed policeman. Zella's eyebrows rose when he removed his cap and set it down.

"Can I help you?" Ivy asked.

"I'm investigating an attack on a—" he flipped open his notepad "—Mr. Walraven. We understand you saw him on Wednesday."

A chill skirted up Ivy's spine, and her hands gripped the counter. "Yes, I saw William at a neighborhood meeting. What's happened? Is he all right?"

"His name isn't William, it's Robert, and this morning he was attacked in Madison Square Park."

Not Will, but Bert. Ivy gasped, and her hand flew to her mouth.

"He was taken to New York Hospital but remains unconscious."

"Who would do such a thing?" Ivy's gaze turned to her aunt, and Zella put an arm around her shoulders.

"That's what I'm hoping you'd tell me. Did you find anyone to be particularly hostile toward him at that meeting?"

"You don't think one of the shop owners in this neighborhood did this, do you?"

"We're checking multiple lines of inquiry."

"No," Ivy shook her head. "I didn't notice any hostility toward Robert directly. People were understandably upset about the Walravens' department store, but the mood was congenial by the time the meeting ended."

"All right. That's it for now. Please let us know if you hear anything at all that might help us catch the attacker." The policeman closed his notebook and left the store. Ivy locked the door behind him. Her hand shook as she fingered the cameo at her neck.

"I'll go give this food to your grandmother and let her know we're going to the hospital. See if there's anything we can do. The hospital's not far." Zella moved to Ivy's side and laid a hand on her arm. "William probably needs a friendly face right now. We can walk there. It will be quicker than finding a hack at this time of day."

While Zella went upstairs, Ivy grabbed her reticule and slipped a hat on her head and gloves on her hands. Zella returned with Gran trailing behind.

"Please tell William we're praying for his brother," Gran said.

"What if he doesn't want me there?" Ivy's voice was a mere whisper.

"Why wouldn't he want you?" Zella asked.

"I was so upset that he lied to me about his business here that I told him I didn't want any more to do with him."

"He lied?" Zella's eyebrows rose.

"A lie by omission." Even to Ivy's ears, it didn't sound like a good enough reason to push the man out of her life.

"Nevertheless, they need you now, as I'm sure they don't know many people in the city. Stay as long as you need. I'll be fine here," Gran said with a wave.

They arrived at the hospital within fifteen minutes and asked to see Robert.

The nurse manning the front desk stood. "What's your name? I need to check with his relative before I can show you back."

"Of course. It's Mrs. Zella Capp and Miss Ivy King. We'll wait right over here." Zella guided Ivy to stand by a wall near the entry.

Ivy's gaze followed the nurse down the hall. Soon, a door opened, and Will stepped out. His hair looked like he'd run his hands through it, and it stuck up in a few places. His tie lay loose around his neck.

Ivy rushed to his side. "How is he?" She wanted desperately to pull him in for a comforting embrace.

"He's pretty beaten up. The doctor says the injuries to his torso and legs will heal. It's his head they're worried about."

"His head?"

"Yes. Whoever did this gave him a hard enough blow that he's yet to regain consciousness." Will's fists clenched at his sides, and his jaw ticked. "How did you know we were here?"

"A policeman came by the shop."

He ran a hand down his face and Ivy placed a hand on his arm, gently guiding him to a nearby bench.

Once seated, he leaned his head against the wall. Ivy and Zella sat on either side of him, and Ivy clasped his hand. "Is there anything we can do for you? Get you something to eat, perhaps?" Ivy asked.

"No, I'm not hungry." Will squeezed Ivy's hand and released it. "But I'm so glad you're here."

Zella's downcast face surely mirrored Ivy's own as a feeling of helplessness washed over her. All she had to offer were her prayers.

———

Will spent the first twenty-four hours pacing the halls or sitting outside Bert's hospital room, bracing himself for any update. When Ivy and her aunt arrived that first afternoon, he could hardly believe they'd come. They brought a pillow, blanket, and sandwiches from home—small comforts that made the waiting a bit easier.

The hospital staff was kind, though they offered little more than a gentle warning that these things take time. Ivy remained until nightfall, and he eventually hired a cab to take her home. She'd said little, yet her quiet presence was a steady comfort. Together, they prayed for Bert to regain consciousness, and he felt a swell of gratitude for her promise to return.

True to her word, she was back by seven the next morning and returned again today.

Will stretched out the kink in his neck and shifted slightly toward the woman beside him on a hallway bench. Ivy's head was against the wall, but her eyes were open. She must have felt him studying her, because she turned her head and her lips tipped up.

"Thank you for being here," he said.

"Of course. Have you contacted your family? They could be here with you too."

"No. My father has a heart condition, and I worry I may cause him undue stress. If Bert hasn't awoken by tomorrow, I'll let them know."

Ivy pulled off her gloves and captured his hand between hers. How did she know he needed personal contact just now? With his free hand, he rubbed his thumb over her knuckles.

"My hands are calloused," she whispered, not lifting her head.

"They're lovely hands." He meant it. No, she didn't have the soft hands of a woman accustomed to leisure, but they were feminine nonetheless. How much work faced her when she returned home? "I'm worried I'm taking you away from your shop."

"It's Sunday, remember? The shop's not open."

"You missed church."

She smiled. "I'm sure God will understand."

"And you were here yesterday. Was your grandmother okay without you there?"

"The last few Saturdays have been slow, so I don't think she was overrun with customers."

"You have a lot to contend with, just the two of you. I imagine most of it falls on your shoulders, correct?"

"Gran's arthritis makes it difficult for her to spend long hours helping customers or working around the shop. She says she can do more, but I've seen the pain on her face when she thinks I'm not looking."

Will's heart hurt for both women. And for the pain Denwall had caused. "I'm so sorry about not telling you who I was. That my family owns the store that causes you more worry."

"Why did you feel you had to hide it?" Her eyebrows came together in a frown.

Why, indeed? "I didn't want to ruin the pleasure of your company. I hoped you'd get to know me and either like me—or not—for who I am, not what I own."

"But isn't Denwall a part of who you are? It's a piece of the puzzle that makes you the man who sits here now."

He supposed she was right. "Can you forgive me?"

"I already have. It's so much more than just department stores taking our customers that worries me. Our rent will be going up soon and publishers are becoming more difficult to work with because they'd rather do business with the big booksellers. I'm afraid the days of the small shop owner are numbered."

So her rent was going up. He wondered how much, and if he could help without letting her know he was helping. She didn't seem like the type of person who'd take kindly to charity or his interference.

He searched for the right words without sounding like he was placating her. "I understand your concerns. But I think there's still plenty of room for the small shops. You must make sure you offer something unique. As much as I take pride in our company, I know there is a level of intimacy we can't bring to the customer like you can. Chances are the people who man the counters of Denwall won't know their customers by name. Won't form any kind of trusting relationship."

"That's sad."

"I think that when customers come into a place like Denwall, they aren't expecting personalized customer service. They want good customer service, to be sure. They like that all their shopping needs are in one place and the prices are competitive." He paused and tilted his head. "My point is, I don't think Denwall's presence is going to hurt you. You may even find you have more customers who come in looking for something we can't offer."

Ivy nodded. "Maybe you're right. Remember how I told you about my parents' rare book business?"

How could he forget? She'd sparkled like a thousand candles when telling him.

"I've been thinking more about it, trying to figure out how to follow in their footsteps."

Will placed his hand on hers. "I'd be glad to help. Give you some capital to work with to get you started. It's the least I can do."

Tears welled in Ivy's eyes. "Thank you. That's very kind. Probably the kindest offer anyone has ever made me. But I can't accept."

Pride was a formidable foe, but Will was determined to break through Ivy's. He'd make it his mission to help her fulfill her dream.

TWENTY-ONE

Ivy stayed next to Will for most of the afternoon, and he could tell by her posture she was getting tired. He offered to walk her home, but she insisted she'd be fine on her own. Finally, he talked her into letting him get her a cab. For the next hour, he paced the hallway floor. After a while, he couldn't take it anymore and ventured outside for a walk around the block.

When he returned, the front desk nurse stood. "There you are, Mr. Walraven. I've been looking for you."

The hair on the nape of his neck stiffened. "What's happened?"

"Your brother opened his eyes."

"Thank you, thank you." He turned and moved down the hall as fast as he could without breaking into a run.

Will pushed open the door to the dimly lit ward, and his chest expanded with relief at the sight of Bert lying in the narrow bed, eyes blinking.

Although it had been four days since the mugging, it felt like four years had passed since he was told Bert was in the hospital. Will had spent countless hours sitting by Bert's bedside, talking to him as if he could hear, pleading for a sign that his brother's mind would return to them.

And now, as he stood gazing at Bert's pale face and the rise and fall of his chest, he felt a surge of gratitude unlike anything he had ever experienced. Bert was awake and though his expression hinted at confusion, a spark of recognition sent a rush of warmth through Will's veins.

Thank you, Lord.

The doctor bustled into the room, and the nurse shooed Will aside. "Why don't you wait out in the hall, Mr. Walraven. The doctor will talk to you after examining your brother."

After waiting four days to see his brother open his eyes, the last thing he wanted was to wait in the hall again, but Will complied. About twenty minutes later, the nurse beckoned him into the room, and the doctor apprised him of Bert's condition. The best thing for his recovery, the man said, was to take things slow. There was no need to rush. Bert would be in the hospital for at least two more days.

"Bert?" Will asked as he moved toward the bed.

Bert's gaze slowly turned toward him. A faint, weary smile graced his lips, and Will took a hesitant step closer to the bed, his fingers trembling at his sides.

"You're back with us." His voice quivered with emotion.

Bert's lips parted, but no words emerged.

"Are you thirsty?" Will reached for the glass of water by the bedside and brought it to his brother's chapped lips.

Will's vision blurred, and he blinked.

When Bert lay his head on the pillow, Will returned the glass to the stand and sat in a chair beside the bed. He reached out, his hand finding Bert's with a trembling touch. The sensation was real and tangible—the grip of a brother whose strength had always been a constant in his life.

Bert's fingers weakly returned the pressure of his hand. In that simple touch, Will felt the weight of uncertainty lift.

"How are you feeling?"

"A little woozy." Bert closed his eyes, and his chest rose with the effort to take in a deep breath. "What happened? How did I end up here?"

The doctor had said he might wake with some amnesia, but it was alarming that Bert didn't remember the mugging.

"You were attacked in Madison Square Park early Thursday morning."

"What day is it?" Bert's voice sounded hoarse and gritty.

"It's Sunday afternoon. You've been out for almost four days."

Bert's eyes flew open. "Four days? I thought it was a few hours." He palmed the side of his head and winced.

"Does your head hurt?"

"Feels like a hammer hitting my skull."

Concern gripped Will's stomach. "Do you want me to fetch a nurse to give you something for the pain?"

"Not yet." Bert shook his head. "It will make me sleepy, and I feel groggy enough." He turned his head to Will, and his eyes peered at him from underneath the clean white bandage. "I remember someone coming up behind me at the park. Did they rob me?"

"They didn't take anything. I don't know if you put up a good fight or if they were scared off before they got the chance, but you still had your watch on, and your wallet was full of cash when the police arrived."

"They sure gave me a real drubbing for nothing."

The nurse stopped by Bert's bedside, checked his pulse, and took his temperature, jotting the results on a piece of paper clipped to a wooden board.

"How does he look, nurse?" Will asked.

"Everything looks normal." She smiled and patted Bert's hand.

Bert ran a shaky hand over his face, staring at Will. "You look awful, Will, so I can't imagine my appearance."

"Thanks, brother. I can always count on you to tell the unvarnished truth."

"Have you been here this whole time?"

"Most of it. I returned to the hotel occasionally to get some rest."

"Do Mother and Father know I'm here?"

Will shook his head. "If you didn't regain consciousness by tomorrow, I planned to telegram them. The doctor said you weren't in imminent danger, and I worried about Father's heart."

"I would have done the same in your shoes."

"Thanks. That means a lot. Fortunately, the newspapers never got wind of the incident. I was worried that they'd run an article, and someone from Philadelphia might see it and notify Father. But they never did."

"It's good that no one but you and the police know what happened."

Will shifted in his chair. "Well, except for Miss King and her family."

Bert gave him a small smile. "She's forgiven you, then?"

"Yes."

"Good. How did she find out I was here?"

"The police stopped by the bookshop to question them."

Bert's brow furrowed. "What for?"

"They suspected someone from the neighborhood meeting might be holding a strong grudge."

Bert pinched the bridge of his nose. "I guess it's possible. What did Miss King say?"

"She didn't think it likely. She and her aunt stopped by to check on you after the police left the shop on Friday afternoon. They were very worried about you."

"That was kind of them."

"Ivy has been here every day, keeping me company. Praying for you."

Bert's lips turned up. "I like Miss King. I'm glad you're spending more time with her."

"She's a good friend."

Bert's chuckle was followed by a groan. "Don't make me laugh. It hurts."

"What's so funny?"

Bert sighed. "Because I think she is more than a friend." Will started to protest, but Bert raised his hand. "All I'm saying is that she is becoming more important. Am I right?"

"I don't know." Will rubbed a hand down his face. "I enjoy her company. She's intelligent. Kind. But..."

"But what?"

"She lives in New York, and I'm returning to Philadelphia."

Bert touched his temple with a light forefinger, and Will worried that the conversation was overtaxing him. It was certainly giving Will heartburn.

"I think you'll miss it here when you're gone," Bert said. "Besides, what's in Philadelphia that's better?"

Will had been so focused on stepping into Father's shoes, marrying the perfect society wife, that he'd never considered what he'd feel like once he achieved that dream. Right now, the idea sent an ache through his chest. That life sounded like his father's life. Did that also mean he'd end up just like Charles Walraven? Too demanding? Too focused on making more money?

The image of what his life would look like twenty years from now loomed before him like a prison sentence.

So, what would happen if he told his family he didn't want to return to Philadelphia? That he'd decided the life he desired—the woman he desired—resided in Manhattan?

Father would have a conniption fit. That's what would happen.

Fanciful thinking, anyway. He and Ivy hadn't discussed how they felt about each other, let alone marriage. Maybe she was happy with her current situation as an unmarried woman. She wouldn't be the first.

"Will?" Bert had been waiting for an answer.

"I don't know what I want anymore. And even if you're right, and I'm meant to stay here, I'm worried about Father. He'd be furious if he knew I was interested in someone he considered beneath us. It might be the tipping point that causes a heart attack."

"You give yourself too much credit. God is in control of that situation, not you."

He was right, of course. Regardless, Will would never forgive himself if something happened.

"If Ivy's the one, you'll find a way to make it work."

Will rubbed a hand across his chest. He had no idea how she felt, and she might not care for him the same way.

The nurse brought Bert his soup, and he ate every drop. Before long, his eyes drifted closed.

Will turned and beckoned to the nurse. "Is it all right for him to go back to sleep already?"

"It's perfectly fine. He'll be weak for a few days and will tire easily. Why don't you go home and get some rest yourself?"

He was reluctant to leave, but the nurse was correct. Now that Bert was conscious again, Will expected slumber to come more quickly. And he desperately needed a good night's sleep. But instead of going straight to the hotel, Will took the short walk to the bookshop. A light shone from the upstairs window, and he stepped up to the front door and rang the doorbell.

Within a few minutes, Ivy appeared at the door. Her eyes widened, and she hurried to flip the lock.

"Is everything all right?" Her voice trembled as she stood aside to let Will pass.

"I'm on my way back to the hotel. Ivy, I have excellent news!" He grabbed her hands.

"Bert?"

"Yes. He's awake."

Ivy threw her arms around Will's neck. "I'm so glad." Still holding onto his shoulders, she leaned back and looked at his face.

Will's hands sneaked around her waist. He'd been itching to feel her body wrapped in his almost since the moment he met her.

A faint blush crept up her cheeks, but he didn't let her go, even though he knew he should. Every argument he'd made to Bert flew away like a feather in a hurricane.

When she lifted her chin, he lowered his head and placed a gentle, tentative kiss on her full lips. She slid her arms around his neck in an invitation he couldn't resist, and he dove in for more. She tasted of sugar and lemons, sweet and tart, and he wanted to go on tasting her.

For the first time, a woman fit perfectly in his arms.

He reluctantly pulled his lips away and touched his forehead to hers, trying to steady his breathing. "I should go."

"You're welcome to come in. Have a bite to eat with us." Her voice was a whisper.

No encouragement needed. "All right. That sounds good." After four days of constant worry and little appetite, Will was starving.

TWENTY-TWO

Ivy's heart was so light, she thought she might float away. She took Will's hand and led him upstairs. Gran's lips turned up in a wide grin when they came through the door.

"I don't want to intrude," Will said after Ivy explained she'd invited a guest to dinner.

Gran patted Will's arm. "Nonsense. You're skin and bones."

He raised his eyebrows, but Ivy just shrugged. "Who am I to argue?"

"I'm sorry about your brother. How is he faring?"

"I'm happy to report that he regained consciousness this afternoon."

Gran clapped her hands together. "That's wonderful news! Praise the Lord."

They sat around the small kitchen table, barely fitting in the small space. Ivy could imagine this was an experience Will had never had before, coming from such a wealthy family. Her finger ran over a tiny hole in the worn tablecloth. She moved her cup to cover the spot and then thought better of it. This was her life, holes and all, and she wasn't ashamed of it.

However, Will soon had her relaxing and encouraged Gran to

share stories of her childhood in England, their move to America to run a farm, and how she moved in with her son and daughter-in-law when her husband died.

"Did your parents grow up in Philadelphia, William?" Gran asked.

He wiped his mouth with a napkin. "My mother's family were merchants from Boston, but my father's father was a bank manager in Philadelphia."

"Your father didn't want to follow in his father's footsteps, I take it?"

"My father was more interested in being a merchant, like his father-in-law. And then he met James Dennison, who helped in his father's tailor shop. They became friends and pooled their resources, including a loan from my grandfather, to open a dry goods store."

Gran's eyebrows shot up. "How did they grow to such a large establishment?"

"As a teenager, my father traveled with his family to Europe and was fascinated with stores like the Bon Marché in Paris and A.T. Stewart's here in New York. He wanted to emulate their model of lavish stores reminiscent of palaces. James appreciated the idea of a store with a wide variety of merchandise divided into distinct departments. He envisioned an emporium where a woman could find everything she needed in one place." He chuckled. "For the first store, James tempered my father's enthusiasm for an establishment too luxurious for them to afford. But then they grew and could invest more money in the stores."

"My, what a story!" Gran said.

Ivy stopped eating, her fork and knife suspended above her plate. "You never stop to think how something like a shop comes into being, but we all start somewhere. With an idea or a need to fill." She shrugged a shoulder. "I assumed Denwall had been passed down through a line of wealthy Walravens. I'm sorry for that. I see now the hard work that went into building and growing something that started as an idea of two young men."

"It's not unlike starting a small bookshop, it would seem. Your heart and soul poured into the endeavor." Gran placed a hand on Ivy's hand. "Your parents put everything they had into this store." She sighed and looked at Will. "Opening your first store in New York is a lot of responsibility on your shoulders."

"It is. But it's what I was prepared to do."

Ivy wondered at this response. It sounded like something Will had recited often to himself. But it also lacked warmth, making her heart ache for him.

Despite their current difficulties, she loved her life as a bookseller. From the excitement of receiving a new shipment from a publisher—especially the work of a new author—to the satisfaction of helping a customer discover a new book. She couldn't imagine herself doing anything else—being anywhere else.

"And what will you do when the store is open?" Gran asked.

Good question. Ivy had not thought that far ahead. Would Will be returning to Philadelphia soon? The idea made her chest ache.

He hesitated, and his eyes searched her face. For a second, she thought he might say he planned to stay in Manhattan, and her heart took flight.

Only to drop like a stone from the top of a building when he looked at Gran and answered, "I'll return to Philadelphia. My father is retiring, and the board will announce his replacement soon."

She swallowed past the knot in her throat and strove to keep her voice light. "I'm assuming it will be you?"

Will nodded. "It appears so. His partner has been pushing for that. And Bert doesn't want anything to do with it."

"But you do?" Of course he did. Someone like him—ambitious, smart, handsome—he'd want it all.

"It's all I've ever wanted. Of course, not at the expense of my father's health. But I figured one day he would retire no matter what, and I would take over. From the moment I understood what Denwall was to our family, I prepared myself to run the business. I worked every position I could at the store."

She tried to smile, but her face felt stiff. "Like stock boy?"

"Of course. I worked in sales and even spent a few weeks in the women's department."

"Oh, I would have liked to have seen that." Gran's mouth turned up in a wry grin.

"I know a lot about women's passions now."

"So, who will run the New York department store?" Ivy asked, although she really didn't have the heart to probe any further into Will's future plans.

"In a few weeks, we'll start our hiring process. We've been conducting interviews to find a general manager and managers for each department. Then they will oversee hiring their own people."

Ivy marveled at the amount of responsibility resting on his shoulders. "The newspaper article said you're hiring close to five hundred employees."

"When we're fully functional."

"You're bringing a lot of opportunities into the area then," Gran said.

"Yes, I want the enterprise to benefit Denwall and the city of New York. I'm sorry if it hurts your business however."

Gran dabbed her mouth with her napkin. "I'm not completely convinced that it will. But time will tell."

Ivy stared at Gran. Was she right? So far, the incoming department store had increased traffic to their bookstore, just as Will predicted it would. Nevertheless, she wasn't ready to strike up the band just yet.

After dinner, Will and Ivy put the dishes in the kitchen. She grabbed a clean dishtowel, filled the sink with soap and water, and began scrubbing the dirty plates. He slipped the towel from her shoulder and took on the task of drying the ones she set on the drainboard.

She wondered about James Dennison, the creative mind behind Denwall. "So, tell me, does your father's partner have any children?"

Will took a wet roasting pan from her hand. "He has a son and four daughters. Their mother died about fifteen years ago, and James only just remarried last year."

"Four daughters—my, my. There must be one or two close to your age." Ivy gave him a cheeky grin. "Did you ever court one of them?" She fervently hoped he hadn't.

"Not on your life. It would be like courting my sister."

Ivy tucked her chin and dipped her hands back in the sink's soapy water. "Looks like we're done."

"That wasn't too bad."

"It's much easier with two people pitching in, and I must say, the time flew by."

Will glanced at his watch. "I should be going." He followed Ivy into the parlor, where her grandmother sat with a book. "Thank you so much for the invitation. It's been a while since I've had a home-cooked meal."

"You're most welcome." Gran took Will's outstretched hand and clasped it in both of her aged ones. "Why don't you walk William downstairs, Ivy?"

Will followed Ivy down the narrow staircase. Inside the shop, moonlight shone through the front window.

She unlocked the door and turned to say goodbye. He stood mere inches away, and she raised her eyes to search his face. The warmth of his nearness, the intensity in his eyes, made her forget to breathe. If she stood on tiptoes, she could brush her lips across his. She'd wanted another kiss since the moment the first one stopped.

Her heart argued that it would be another lovely memory to keep her warm at night.

Her mind told her kissing him again would only make things worse when they parted in a few weeks.

Clearing her throat, she stepped back. "I'll stop by the hospital tomorrow on my way from the library."

"Would you like to have a quick picnic in the park with me?" Will asked. "I'll pick up lunch."

"I think I can spare an hour after work. A picnic sounds lovely."

Will flagged down a cab and gave her a slight wave as he climbed inside.

Ivy waved at him from the sidewalk. It was hard enough to say goodbye for a few hours. How would she bear it when he left for good?

Twenty-Three

Eager to see a recovering Bert for herself, Ivy went straight to the hospital after her shift ended at the library. The nurse at the front desk recognized her and waved. "Mr. Walraven awoke yesterday."

"Yes, I heard. Isn't it wonderful news?"

"It certainly is. Why don't you go back and say hello?"

Ivy moved down the now-familiar long hallway and peeked into Bert's ward. He sat in a chair beside his bed as a nurse removed his bandage. Will wasn't in the room, and Ivy tried to tamp down the disappointment. Bert's lips turned up in a smile when she entered the room. "Good afternoon, Miss King."

"Hello, Mr. Walraven. It's so good to see you awake."

The nurse finished cleaning the gash on Bert's head, and instead of replacing the full head wrap, she taped a square piece of gauze over the healing wound. When she moved away, Ivy stepped into her place.

"You need to call me Bert, as I understand you've been here every day," he said.

"Bert, it is, then."

"Pull up a chair. I'd do it for you, but I'm still a bit woozy, and the nurse has forbidden me to get up. She might clobber me if I did."

Ivy laughed and dragged over a vacant chair. "We wouldn't want that now, would we?"

"Will's not here yet, I'm afraid."

Ivy met Bert's keen eyes. "That's all right. I came to check on you, anyway."

"That's very kind. My brother stopped by this morning but had to meet our foreman at the store at nine." Bert paused and grinned like a Cheshire cat. "He seemed awfully chipper."

Ivy looked at her lap and tried to hide the warmth that bloomed on her face. "Yes, he's so glad you're on the mend." Before Bert could ask questions, she shifted the direction of the conversation.

"How are you feeling, other than the wooziness?"

"It feels good to get that wrapping off." Bert ran a finger lightly over his head. "I don't have the pounding headache I had when I woke up yesterday."

"That's good news. Do you remember what happened that morning you were attacked?"

"Snippets are coming back. It was a man, but I never saw his face."

"But the police say he didn't take anything from you?"

"No, he left everything in my wallet, and my watch was still on my wrist. Not much of a mugger, if you ask me. That watch would've fetched a pretty penny." Bert rubbed his temple. "I wish I'd gotten a better look at him. It all happened so fast. He came up from behind me as I was sitting down. I tried to fight him off, but he had the advantage of surprise. I just remember him pushing me to the ground and kicking me."

Ivy's hand flew to her mouth, and tears pooled in her eyes. "How awful. I'm so sorry, Bert." Why would anyone want to hurt this man? None of it made any sense.

"I think he was warning me," Bert continued, "but I don't

remember exactly. Then he hit me over the head, and that's the last thing I recall until I woke up here yesterday."

"I'm guessing more will come back to you in the coming days."

This wasn't a random attack. He was someone's target.

Bert reached for a glass of water, and Ivy rushed to his side to help him, guiding the cup to his lips.

"Hey, what's this?"

Ivy's eyes darted to the door at the sound of Will's voice, and her heart somersaulted.

"I'm sorry, Miss King, but I've yet to learn how to drink through my nose," Bert muttered.

"Oh, I'm sorry, Bert." Flustered, she dabbed at his face with the corner of his sheet.

"Serves you right for acting too infirm to get your water yourself." Will stepped into the room, and Ivy took a deep breath, trying to calm her racing heart.

"How's the work coming along at the building?" Bert asked as he took the cup from Ivy.

Did he notice how her hand shook?

"It's coming along. Slower than I'd like, but Owens is still confident we'll open on time."

"I wish there was something I could do." Bert groaned and his gaze swept the room. "Plus, I'm dying to get out of this place." When the pretty nurse stationed on the ward looked up from her desk by the door, Bert added, "No offense, nurse. The staff here is wonderful."

Will huffed. "You've just come out of a four-day coma. You'll be in here for a few more days." At the sound of approaching footsteps from the hall, Will turned toward the door. "Here's your doctor now. You can confirm that yourself."

"Good afternoon," the doctor said as he approached Bert's bed. "Let's have a look at that hard head of yours."

Bert grumbled at the doctor's quip.

Will placed a hand on Bert's blanket-covered leg. "I'm going to take Miss King on a picnic, but I won't be too long."

Bert winked at Ivy. "Take your time."

Will's arm felt solid beneath Ivy's hand as they strolled down the bustling sidewalk. They passed an older woman sweeping the stoop of a bakery. She looked up and her lips turned into a knowing smile—the kind reserved for sweethearts out for a stroll.

Ivy glanced away, her cheeks warming. The idea they might look like a couple in love unsettled and thrilled her all at once.

Will seemed unaware of the attention, though his grin hadn't faded since they'd left the hospital. When they reached the park, he gestured toward a shaded spot beneath large oak trees in the park's heart. "There are some nice spots over there."

The gravel crunched softly beneath their feet, and the trees formed a canopy overhead, dappling the path with patches of sunlight. They passed families enjoying picnics, couples stealing quiet moments beneath the shade of old oaks, and children darting about in carefree play.

They found a flat, shaded area, and Ivy helped Will spread out the blanket—looking suspiciously like one from the Holland House hotel with its monogrammed *HH*—on the grass. He placed the basket at one end and then held out his hand to help her sit.

"You couldn't ask for a more perfect day for a picnic," she said as he knelt beside the picnic basket.

Will's eyes searched her face, his gaze lingering on her lips. "Nor better company."

If she leaned forward a little, she could press her lips to his to show how much she agreed with him. Her body swayed of its own volition.

A mother's sharp admonition to her son to stop chasing the ducks stopped Ivy from making a fool of herself.

Will's mouth quirked in a knowing smile.

They unpacked the basket together, laying out an array of sandwiches, fresh fruit, and pastries. Will poured lemonade from a glass bottle into two tin cups, handing one to Ivy.

"Here's to a lovely day," he said, raising his cup in a toast.

"And to the blessing of Bert's recovery," Ivy added, clinking her cup against his. They both sipped, savoring the tart sweetness of the lemonade.

Ivy was hungrier than she realized, and she dug into her sandwich. As they ate, she couldn't help but steal glances at Will. His handsome looks made her wonder if he'd taken other women on picnics during his time away from home.

"Is this your first picnic in New York?" The question tumbled from her lips before she could stop it. Heat rose to her cheeks.

Will looked up from his plate, and his eyes took in their surroundings. "I haven't had time to enjoy New York other than our trip to Central Park."

Ivy's heart soared at the news he hadn't spent his free time with anyone else. Of course, he could be just telling her what she wanted to hear. She tamped down the distrust that Will didn't deserve. Despite his subterfuge about his reasons for being in the city, she believed him to be a man of integrity. "If you get the chance, spend the day at Prospect Park."

"I've heard about it. You can take boats on the water, right?"

"Yes. I haven't been in several years, but it's a lovely place. You said you rowed in college, right?"

Will dusted the pastry crumbs from his hands onto the grass. "You have an excellent memory. I rowed all four years, as did Bert. It's a family tradition."

"Did you like it?"

"An astute question." He tugged at a blade of grass and twiddled it between his fingers. "There are traditions in the Walraven family that one does out of duty, and not all are enjoyable. During my freshman year, I lived on campus and found I liked the freedom of being away from my father's watchful eye. Although I love to row, it's a disciplined sport, and I didn't particularly like the early morning practices. Especially after a night of revelry."

Ivy studied Will's face. "I can't imagine you like that. You're so serious now."

"That year is what my parents refer to as Will's Year of Rebellion." Will's eyes twinkled. "I even got arrested once."

Arrested? Zella's crazy idea of the Walravens being con men flitted through her mind.

Will's belly shook with laughter. "You should see the expression on your face! Not to worry. The incident isn't as bad as it sounds."

She exhaled a long breath. "So, what happened?"

"On one particularly festive evening, a group of us decided it would be fun to steal the opposing team's mascot."

"Which was?"

"A goat."

Ivy's laugh rang out, and she covered her mouth with her hand. "Oh, my. What did you do with the goat, pray tell?"

"We treated Lancelot very well, I'll have you know. He got a better dinner from us than he would have in his own pen." Will removed his hat and ran a hand through his hair. "It's getting warm out here."

"Why don't you take off your jacket?" Once he shrugged out of the coat, she folded it neatly and laid it beside her.

"Thank you. Anyway, the police showed up the next morning and decided it would be grand to arrest the men involved."

"How did they figure out who the culprits were?"

"One of the team members squealed like a stuck pig." Will shrugged one shoulder. "Can't blame him. His charges were dropped." He shifted his arms behind him and leaned back on his forearms. His long legs stretched out and crossed at the ankles.

Ivy's insides fluttered as Will's muscles bunched underneath his snowy white shirt. The sunlight glinted off his hair, highlighting coppery streaks. He'd loosened his necktie and unfastened the top button of his shirt, exposing the valley between his collarbones. Her hands itched to touch the spot, and she squirmed. "So, then what happened?"

"My father had to come to the station and bail me out. Word got out quickly, and he took a lot of ribbing from Philadelphia society for the next month."

"The incident seems harmless enough," Ivy said. "Rather funny, actually."

"My father often lacks a sense of humor. In his defense, it wasn't just the arrest. It was a culmination of things. My grades were horrible. It wasn't my finest moment."

"But look at you now. An upstanding citizen in charge of the newest Denwall store. Your father must be proud of you."

He gave her a sardonic grin. "We'll see. This position is a test."

"What do you mean?"

"Father wants to see if I'm worthy of stepping into his shoes."

Ivy tilted her head, and she studied him. "Is that what you really want? To step into his shoes?"

"I've always believed so."

"You'll put your soul into opening the New York store to leave it behind in someone else's care. Will that be difficult?"

He stared at her for a few seconds, his eyes hooded. "Bert's asked me the same question. Honestly, I hadn't thought about it before because I've known all along that we'd hire a general manager to take over when Bert and I return to Philadelphia."

Ivy stared at the canopy of leaves above her head. That Will would leave once the store officially opened made her want to weep at the disappointment of it all. She'd met a man she could see spending the rest of her life with.

Unfortunately, he had the potential to break her heart in a way she hated to contemplate.

Will stole a glance at the woman beside him. Strands of her hair escaped from beneath the wide-brimmed straw hat trimmed with ribbon, perfectly framing her heart-shaped face. The necklace she toyed with in moments of unease adorned a lace-edged collar. She tipped her head back, face to the sun. A small smile lifted her lips, and she closed her eyes, contentment radiating from her.

When was the last time he enjoyed a leisurely lunch in the middle of a workday? From the moment he graduated from college, he'd put almost every ounce of energy into climbing the Denwall ladder. How had he had time to court Elizabeth Blake? No wonder he didn't know her as well as he thought.

Maybe Bert was onto something by taking time to do the things he loved. Although their father might call him lazy, Bert was one of the hardest workers Will knew. He just had the innate ability to balance out his life.

Ivy opened her eyes and her smile slipped. "You must be eager to get back to work."

Was he? Until the meeting with Owens that morning, he hadn't thought about Denwall in the last few days. The importance of it had diminished considerably. "Our foreman is on top of things. He's a good man."

His eyes took in their surroundings, from the arch that Ivy told him commemorated the centennial of George Washington's inauguration as president to the large fountain serving as a focal point for the park. Across the grassy lawn, a group of boys played catch with a baseball.

Ivy grinned as one lad did a little dance when he caught a fly ball. "Where did you go to play baseball as a child?"

He had only mentioned the sport in passing, yet she remembered. Will loved that about her—that she remembered the small things about people. At church, Ivy had asked parishioners, especially the older ones, specific questions about their lives. Like how a grandchild fared in their first week of school or if a husband had recovered from gout. Faces lit up at her inquiries because she took the time to remember these details.

"If we were in the city, we played at the park across the street from our house. In the country, we played in the backyard."

Ivy's eyebrow quirked. "You have two houses?"

"My parents do, yes."

The muscles in Will's neck tensed. He wasn't comfortable talking about his family's wealth when it appeared she was on the brink of financial disaster.

"You are indeed blessed."

At that moment, he agreed he was the most fortunate man in the world.

"So, tell me about your life in Philadelphia. Do you live with your parents?"

Will ran a hand behind his neck. "No. I bought a house of my own last spring."

"What's it like?"

"It's a townhouse. A brown brick Italianate with tall windows and wrought iron railed balconies. Four stories. There's a pretty little garden in the back."

Ivy sighed. "It sounds lovely. I wish we had a garden." Her brows pinched in thought. "Your house will be perfect for a family."

He'd felt the same way when he purchased the home.

Now, he owed it to Ivy to tell her about Elizabeth. "I bought it for my future wife, Elizabeth. Elizabeth Blake."

"Oh, I see."

The hurt in her voice made him regret his decision to tell her. He searched the branches above his head for the right words to put her mind at ease. "She and I talked at length about getting married. I planned to ask her father for her hand at my father's retirement ball in May and announce our engagement that night."

Ivy's eyes didn't waver from his face, and she didn't interrupt.

He took a deep breath, embarrassed to admit he'd been jilted. "Elizabeth never showed."

Leaning forward, Ivy put her hand on his arm. "That's awful. Why didn't she come? Was she in an accident?"

It didn't surprise him she would assume the best of a woman she didn't know. "She left the country to marry a British aristocrat instead. I imagine she'll be Countess Cumbria by the end of the year."

"Oh, Will. I'm so sorry. Were you heartbroken?"

"More embarrassed than anything. The rejection dinged my pride, but in retrospect, not my heart."

"If that's the case, you were probably lucky she changed her mind." Ivy nodded in that practical way of hers.

She unfolded her legs and laid back on the blanket, eyes on the blue sky.

Will rolled onto his side and propped his head in his hand, bringing him closer. Her nearness made him lightheaded. The hint of honeysuckle that always seemed to linger on her wrapped around him like a gentle caress. It would take only the slightest effort to lean over and kiss her senseless. Make her feel cherished and loved. Maybe even protected.

For the first time, something other than Denwall gave his life purpose.

Twenty-Four

The days were getting shorter, and Ivy knew the walk to the library would soon be shrouded in darkness. Like every morning, Gran accompanied her downstairs to the shop's front door.

Dickens padded after them, tail wagging, as Ivy slipped on a light jacket, reinserting a few loose pins in her hair before placing a hat atop her head. Remembering the Sunday newspaper's prediction of rain, she grabbed her umbrella.

"Wait! I need to give you something before I forget again." Gran moved behind the counter and retrieved an envelope from a drawer under the register. "Getting old isn't fun. I'd forget my head if it weren't attached to my neck."

Ivy accepted the envelope Gran handed her, noting the thick paper and elegant handwriting. It was addressed to her, as well as to Gran and Zella, and was sealed with a wax stamp—a bold and elegant *W*. Breaking the seal carefully, she pulled out the most ornate invitation she'd ever seen, its edges trimmed in gold embossing.

You are cordially invited to Denwall's Grand Opening Ball on October Nineteenth.

Ivy's chest tightened. She'd never been to a glamorous ball. A few dances, yes, but she'd always sat with the wallflowers, too embarrassed by her limp to join in.

She couldn't turn the invitation down—it was to be Will's moment in the sun—and she couldn't refuse to dance if he asked. Could she find a dress that wouldn't cost a fortune yet was glamorous enough to wear to such a fancy affair?

What about her shoes? Ivy glared down at the ugly platformed boot that kept her gait steady. She swallowed past the lump in her throat. In her lifetime, she'd cried far too many tears over how the Lord had seen fit to create her. This time, there'd be no waterworks. She'd straighten her shoulders and force herself to walk into the ballroom with her head high and a smile on her face.

Maybe Zella would have some ideas about how to remake one of Ivy's dresses into a ballgown. Or perhaps Mrs. Dixon, who'd been kind enough to welcome Ivy into her home, could loan her one of her daughter's hand-me-downs.

Yes, she'd stoop that low to avoid embarrassing Will in front of his family and friends—and so he wouldn't easily forget her when he returned to Philadelphia.

"You'll go, won't you?" Gran asked, clearly sensing her hesitation.

"Yes, of course."

"Oh, look. There's William now." Gran padded to the front door and unlocked it.

Ivy kissed her on the cheek and scooted out the door. "See you this afternoon."

"Good morning," Will greeted her warmly as Gran locked the shop door behind her and waved goodbye. This was the sixth consecutive workday that he'd shown up to join her on her way to work.

Like every time before, her heart fluttered like a thousand butterflies had taken flight in her chest. "Hello, there."

She loved how he smelled first thing in the morning, like shaving balm and soap. His square jaw was freshly shaven, and his hair was combed neatly. He was, in a word, dapper. Every detail about him, from the shine on his shoes to the way he tipped his hat, exuded a kind of effortless elegance that made her insides quiver with longing.

"How was your day…" they began at the same time and laughed. This had become their routine. Each would recount the day before.

"You go first," Will insisted.

"There's not much to tell. Busy. How's Bert doing?"

"He's fine. Back from Philadelphia."

"If your mother is anything like mine was, she probably pampered him to death."

Will chuckled. "After she threatened to kill him for getting himself mugged."

"He's not planning on taking trips to the park any time soon, is he?" The thought of Bert wandering to the park again made her insides churn. She couldn't shake the image of him lying unconscious in that hospital bed.

"No. Even though the police have assured him the attacker is unlikely to strike again, we think it's best to lie low for a while."

"Has he remembered anything else from the morning he was mugged?"

Will nodded. "Yes, he has. Something the man said."

"The attacker said something?" Did he ask him to hand over his wallet and Bert refused?

Will hesitated as though he was reluctant to tell her. He let out a huff. "He said something like, 'Keep your mouth shut.'"

Goosebumps raised the hair on Ivy's arms. The warning convinced her that Bert's mugging was neither random nor a botched robbery. "Do you really believe that someone would try to hurt him again?"

"I don't know. But he's a grown man tired of being cooped up." Will shoved his hands in his pockets. "All I can do is pray that he stays safe."

"Here we are," Ivy said at the bottom of the library's steps. She dipped her chin and stared at her feet. "Thank you for the invitation. We received it yesterday."

"You'll come, won't you?"

She pulled in a fortifying breath and lifted her face to meet his eyes. "Yes. Of course."

He looked around, stepped closer until their bodies brushed, and took her hand in his. His eyes searched her face and lingered on her lips. "I'll miss you today," he whispered. "I'm finding it harder and harder to concentrate on work when my mind's on you."

"I have the same affliction," she whispered back.

"If we weren't standing on a busy sidewalk, I might be tempted to kiss you."

Warmth spread like honey in her belly. "I might let you."

He lifted her gloved hand and brushed a kiss across her knuckles. "I wish there were more hours in a day to spend with you, but at least we have our morning walks." He stepped back and said, "I haven't had the chance to visit your library yet. Do you mind if I come in and look around? See where you work?"

Not only did she not mind, but her heart soared that he wanted to. "That would be lovely. But can you come back later? Mr. Collins won't allow you in the library until we're officially open."

"I'll be back later, then." He waved and moved down the sidewalk, his stride quick and purposeful.

The next three hours flew by. The library bustled with activity, students and scholars filling the study carousels, their heads bent over books and papers. The visitors were more needy than usual, and Ivy spent much of the morning assisting researchers and retrieving books from closed stacks.

"Excuse me, miss. Can you help me find a book on the feeding habits of the Peruvian Mock-Pigeon." The deep voice came from directly behind her.

Ivy stifled a laugh and turned to find Will standing close, a cheeky grin on his face. "I'm sorry, sir. I've never heard of such a bird."

His lips turned down in a pout. "Oh, well, I guess I'll just look around, then."

He strolled in and out of the rows of books. Every so often, he'd catch her watching him, and he'd toss her a sweet smile.

Her task of reshelving misplaced books had never been so much fun.

Ivy returned to her desk for another armload, when a movement across the library made her stop and stare.

Jack McGill—the man she didn't doubt had sold Bert the Defoes.

The stolen Defoes.

Her pulse thrummed. Why hadn't she thought of it before?

If Bert had yet to identify McGill to the police, there would be a strong reason for the thief to want to prevent that from happening. Was this man Bert's attacker? She took a deep breath, steadying herself.

She found Will and pulled him behind some books.

"I'm not sure we should be kissing in the library," he teased.

"Don't look now, but across the room is the man I believe Bert purchased his Defoes from. Jack McGill. I can't believe I didn't think of it earlier, but it would make sense that he might have wanted to warn Bert before he talked to the police, don't you think?"

Will's eyes widened. "You could be right. With everything that happened in the park, we forgot about the stolen books. Bert never talked to the police."

Ivy studied Jack McGill—if that was his real name. The man had a peculiar way of moving, like he was always on the lookout, constantly scanning his surroundings. He flipped through books with an air of nonchalance but looked up often as if calculating his next move.

She grabbed Will's arm. "I think he's going to steal another book."

"I'll keep an eye on him. Why don't you go back to your desk, so he doesn't get suspicious?"

Without being too obvious, Will kept a close watch on McGill while Ivy went about her work. If she believed this McGill was the one Bert had purchased the stolen Astor books from, Will didn't doubt her.

McGill wandered in and out of several alcoves, sometimes bringing volumes back to the table only to get up again a few minutes later. However, his favorite spot appeared to be the rare books section on the far left. The table he returned to offered an excellent view of the alcove, likely allowing him to ensure it remained empty of visitors.

Yet, he stole nothing.

McGill stood and gathered his belongings, including a bulky coat—too bulky for the late summer weather they'd experienced the past three days.

A grandfather clock on the floor below struck twelve. Ivy's shift ended at noon if Will wasn't mistaken.

Just when Will thought McGill had decided to move on, he saw him slip a thin volume inside his coat pocket and turn toward the stairs.

Ivy must have seen it, too, because she was at Will's side in an instant.

He laid a hand on her shoulder. "Stay here. I'll follow him."

"Oh no, you don't. I'm coming." The look in her eyes convinced him she wouldn't be left behind. He needed to stay on the thief before he lost sight of him altogether. He'd just have to make sure Ivy remained safe.

They trailed closely behind McGill as he headed down the stairs and outside the library. Now the books were officially stolen property.

Will took Ivy's hand and pulled it through the crook of his arm.

She peeked up at him. "What are you going to do?"

"We need to flag down a patrolman, so keep an eye out, but I don't want to lose sight of McGill." He also wanted to ensure the thief didn't ditch his coat.

McGill strolled leisurely, presumably to avoid attracting attention. Following him wasn't difficult and neither was finding a police officer, given the affluent, well-patrolled area. At the next block, Ivy pointed to two of New York's finest, clad in knee-length navy greatcoats and cloth-covered helmets.

"You go tell them what's going on, and I'll keep trailing McGill."

She nodded and moved toward the patrolmen with a speed that belied her bad leg. Will couldn't help but smile. She had courage and pluck like no other woman he'd ever met.

Ivy returned to Will's side, her eyes gleaming. "I think we've got him."

He loved the way she grinned at the excitement of it all.

One of the patrolmen strode forward and clamped a hand around McGill's arm. But McGill wasn't going down without a fight. He twisted sharply, shoving the officer to the ground before bolting—straight toward Ivy.

Without hesitation, she stuck out her thick-soled boot. McGill stumbled but continued running.

Ivy's quick thinking bought Will the moment he needed, and he launched into a sprint. McGill wasn't slipping away—not after everything Bert had been through.

McGill darted into an alley, his coat flapping behind him.

Will's feet pounded against the cobblestones, narrowing the gap between them.

"Stop!" His voice cut through the air like a whip. McGill glanced over his shoulder, his eyes wide with panic. But instead of stopping, he pushed over a stack of crates to block Will's path.

Will leaped over the crates, his shoes scraping against the wood. The thief darted around another corner but lost some momentum. With a final burst of effort, Will lunged forward, catching the man's arm and spinning him around.

"Let me go!" McGill snarled, thrashing like a caged animal. He drove his fist into Will's ribs, forcing a grunt from him. Will stumbled back a step, but his eyes never left McGill's.

"I'm not letting you get away with this," Will said, his voice low and unyielding.

McGill lunged, aiming to bowl Will over, but Will sidestepped and grasped him around the waist. They crashed to the ground, the impact jarring but satisfying as Will pinned McGill beneath him. McGill's head connected with Will's jaw, but Will's strength held firm.

Hurried footsteps echoed in the alley, and Will glanced up to see the patrolmen rushing toward them. One of the officers took hold of McGill's arm and yanked him from the ground. "Let's see what you have in your pockets," he said.

McGill struggled against the patrolman's hold. "Let go of me. I don't have anything in my pockets!"

The officers patted down the jacket, and McGill's shoulders slumped in defeat as the older patrolman pulled three books from a hidden lining. Flipping them open, he nodded grimly. "They're from the Astor Library, all right. Let's take him to the station."

Still breathing hard, but on his feet, Will bent and rested his hands on his knees. He turned his head to find Ivy standing at the edge of the alley, her arms hugging her waist, and her face pale.

The younger patrolman clapped handcuffs onto McGill's wrists. "Miss King, we'll need you and your friend to come with us to give a formal statement."

"Certainly." Ivy's hand shook as she pushed a loose tendril from her face.

Will put an arm around her shoulders and pulled her in tight.

She tipped her chin and searched his face, her eyes roaming over every feature. "Are you all right?" Her words came out in a whisper.

Will slipped his other arm around her and tucked her head under his chin. "I'm fine." Truth be told, his jaw and ribs burned like they were on fire. "He didn't stand a chance."

He felt her chuckle all the way to his toes. "I didn't think he did." She moved away, and he immediately missed her warmth.

On tiptoe, she brushed a kiss across his cheek. "William Walraven, you're my hero."

He held her in place, tight against him, and whispered in her ear, "It was a team effort. I couldn't have done it without you."

He silently thanked God for bringing Ivy into his world. *Lord, I want to be this woman's protector for the rest of our lives.*

TWENTY-FIVE

At the patrolmen's request, Ivy and Will followed them to the police station. Not far from where they stopped McGill, the station house loomed—a no-nonsense red brick building alive with activity. Ivy trailed the officers inside, her senses immediately assaulted by the dim light and the mingled smells of body odor and cigar smoke.

The front of the station featured a long wooden counter resembling a hotel reception desk, complete with cubbyholes in the wall behind it. Seated on a raised platform, the desk sergeant presided over the space with an authoritative air. Despite the tidy layout, the scuffed and scratched counter bore silent witness to the countless cases that had passed through.

The older patrolman introduced himself as Patrolman Nolan and brought McGill forward to stand before the sergeant. Ivy and Will hovered nearby as the younger patrolman relayed the arrest details.

Nolan gestured toward them. "This is Miss Ivy King and Mr. William Walraven. Miss King saw the thief taking the books from the Astor. Mr. Walraven helped us apprehend McGill."

Ivy stepped forward, shoulders squared. "I also believe this thief is connected to the attack on Robert Walraven. Mr. Walraven purchased a set of *Robinson Crusoe* books—which were the property of the Astor—from a man matching Jack McGill's description."

The sergeant gave her a thin-lipped smile. "How do you know all this?" His tone suggested he didn't believe her.

Refusing to be cowed, she met his gaze. "I'm a librarian at the Astor."

The man turned his eyes on Will. "What's your name again, and how are you involved?"

"I'm William Walraven of Denwall Department Stores. I've already spoken to the police about my brother, Robert, who was in the hospital for a week after he was mugged in Madison Square Park—possibly at the hands of this man."

McGill's eyes widened in panic as he struggled against Nolan's grip. "You can't prove that." He glared venomously at Ivy. "Maybe you should check into *her*! That assistant librarian's the inside man, and he's probably roped in some of the women there too."

Mr. Collins was part of the ring? Why didn't that surprise her?

The officers ignored McGill's protests and dragged him toward the cells. The desk sergeant retrieved a sheet of paper from a cubbyhole behind him and slid it across the desk toward Will, along with a pen.

"You and Miss King need to fill this out," he instructed, tapping the paper with his forefinger. "Detail everything about the incident with your brother and today's arrest. Tell us about this assistant librarian too. There's a table over there you can use." He pointed to a two-person table outside the police captain's office.

"Of course." Will turned and settled a hand on Ivy's back.

A man in a loose-fitting suit with a notepad and pencil in hand stepped in front of them. "Excuse me. I'm a reporter from *The Daily New Yorker*, covering the police beat. I couldn't help but overhear your conversation with the sergeant. Can you fill me in on what happened to Robert Walraven and how it involves the arrested man, Jack McGill?"

Will's jaw clenched. Talking to a nosy reporter was probably the last thing he wanted to do. "I'm sorry. I can't comment at this moment."

Like Dickens with a juicy bone, the reporter didn't let go. "Your family is becoming well-known in the city, and the good people of New York deserve to know what you're up to."

"Come to my office in the morning," Will said. "Nine o'clock. I'll tell you what I know then."

"Will do. See you then."

Will ushered Ivy to the table and pulled out a chair for her, his hand lingering briefly on her shoulder. He pulled the second chair close enough that their knees almost touched when he sat down.

She placed a gentle hand on his arm. "I've not considered how your lives must draw attention—both admiration and envy, I imagine. People are obsessed with the comings and goings of the wealthy, if the society columns are any indication. I'm sorry for that. How difficult it must be to live under such scrutiny."

Will covered her hand with his own, his thumb tracing small circles on her wrist. "Most days I hardly notice it anymore," he said softly, his eyes meeting hers. "But lately, I've been thinking about how it might affect those close to me—those I care about."

What was he saying? Was he hinting at a future together, but didn't think she could handle it? "I'm not afraid of what others might think." The words stuck in her throat. "Not when it comes to things that matter."

A smile tugged at the corner of his mouth. "No, you wouldn't be. You're the bravest woman I know, Ivy King. Chasing down book thieves, standing up to skeptical sergeants..."

"All in a day's work." She appreciated the compliment and tried to give him a cheery smile, but an ache traveled from her heart to her stomach and twisted in a knot. She must have misunderstood his concerns about scrutiny. He most likely wasn't referring to her.

"Speaking of work," Will looked at his watch, "your grandmother will be worried that you're not home by now."

Gran! She'd be worried sick. "You're right. I need to get this finished and return home."

After handing over their statement, they stepped out into the afternoon sun. The streets were busy, and Will didn't remove his hand from her back.

"I'll escort you home. After the morning's excitement, I'd feel better seeing you there safely."

"Always the gentleman." She tried for a teasing tone, but it fell flat. Her heart just wasn't in the mood.

——

The walk back to Ivy's home felt like the calm after a storm. The rush of adrenaline had faded, replaced by the lingering ache in Will's ribcage. He stole a glance down at Ivy, who held his arm in a tight grip. She hadn't said much since they'd left the station. What was going around in that lovely head of hers?

By the time they reached the bookshop, Will had already replayed the day's events in his mind a dozen times. From their walk to the library that morning—it felt like days ago now—to McGill's arrest. Ivy's kiss on his cheek and her words that he was her hero were more potent than the sharpest punch that scum could throw.

Their conversation at the station gave him a lot to think about. Was she willing to consider a life with him, immersed in his family, Denwall, and the world of high society maneuverings? Or was she already regretting her bold statement that she wasn't afraid of scrutiny?

Ivy's grandmother met them at the door, her expression a

mixture of relief and worry. "There you are! I've been so worried. I even messaged Zella."

"I'm fine." Ivy stepped into the store and took her grandmother's hand. "I'm sorry I worried you. You, too, Zell." She gave her aunt a small smile. "I'm sorry you came all this way. Aren't you in the middle of a deadline?"

"Yes, but it doesn't matter. It's not like you to be late, and my mind conjured up all sorts of scenarios."

"I can imagine it did." Ivy slipped off her hat and gloves and laid them on the counter.

Zella's gaze landed on Will, and her grey eyes grew wide. "What happened to your jaw?"

Will cringed that they'd have to explain the incident to not one concerned relative, but two. And there'd be no sugarcoating it with Zella and her journalist's instincts.

"We ran into a bit of trouble today."

"That's one way to put it," Ivy murmured, her lips twitching.

"Let's go have a cup of tea then, and you can tell us all about it." Mrs. King shut the door behind them and flipped the sign to *Closed*.

Over tea and freshly made sandwiches, Ivy recounted the day's events. He quirked a smile as she painted a vivid picture of McGill's arrest and the part Will played in it. His actions sounded better coming from her mouth than he remembered them.

"You mean to tell me Ivy threw herself into danger chasing after some ruffian?" Zella asked.

"I wouldn't call it throwing myself into danger." Ivy tilted her head toward Mrs. King and arched her eyebrows as if to tell her aunt to calm down for the older woman's sake. "Will was with me the whole time." She patted her grandmother's hand. "Honestly, Gran. I didn't do anything."

Mrs. King gripped her teacup and shook her head in wonder. "You could have been hurt." She turned a sharp gaze on Will. "In fact, by the way you're nursing that jaw, young man, I'd say you were."

Will touched his jaw instinctively, feeling the tender spot where McGill had landed a glancing blow. "I'll be fine."

Ivy clasped her grandmother's wrinkled hand. "And I promise, I was never in danger. Will protected me, although he didn't want me to leave the library to follow McGill."

The older woman's lips pressed into a thin line, though her eyes softened. "You've always been too stubborn for your own good."

"I take after you, remember?" Ivy said with a smile.

"That you do." Mrs. King returned the smile, though it was tinged with exasperation. "But I've never caught a criminal." Her expression grew thoughtful as she added, "I'm proud of you both. Even if I'm still mad at you."

Will relaxed slightly, letting the warmth of the moment settle over him. Over the last few weeks, he'd come to enjoy his time in this cozy space. He doubted the French chef he'd hired for his new home would allow him in the kitchen, let alone take afternoon tea there.

The conversation turned to the latest local news as they finished their tea. "Ivy, remind me to show you the article later," Mrs. King said, "but this morning's newspaper mentions that Mr. Ashbourne is selling part of his library at an auction at the beginning of November."

Zella patted her lips with her napkin. "I hear he's in dire financial straits. He wouldn't be selling any of his precious collection otherwise." She tapped her chin with her forefinger "Didn't your parents know him, Ivy?"

"Yes, that's right. He often hired them to hunt down books or to assess a book he was considering for his library."

Will leaned back in his chair, watching the comfortable interaction between the women at the table. This kitchen felt more like home than any grand dining room he'd ever sat in.

Ivy sighed. "I'd love to be able to attend the auction. See what he's selling."

But she couldn't get into such an event without a connection or at least an escort. He cleared his throat. "I'll escort you to the auction, if you'd like. With your grandmother or aunt, of course."

Zella arched a brow. "Well, aren't you gallant?"

Mrs. King beamed at William like he was the cleverest man in New York. "It's a splendid idea!"

"It's the least I can do," Will said with a shrug. "Especially after today."

Ivy's blue eyes searched his face. "But Denwall's grand opening is on the nineteenth. I thought you had to return to Philadelphia?"

"I won't be leaving right away. I'll stay a few weeks to make sure the new general manager is settled, and things are running smoothly."

But his plans went far beyond ensuring the store's success. Before he left the city, he intended to ask Ivy to marry him. Where they'd live didn't matter—not to him. They'd figure out those details later. All that mattered was they'd be together. He knew she'd need convincing. She wasn't the type to be easily swayed. But he was an excellent negotiator, and he'd approach this as methodically as any business deal.

He darted a glance at Zella. Her eyes gleamed, and she quirked her lips.

Yes, the woman had a reporter's instincts.

TWENTY-SIX

The following Friday, the Astor library buzzed with excitement at the news that the head librarian had an important visitor. When word got to the second floor that they'd exited his office, Ivy joined the other librarians at the banister, peering down to the main floor below. Mr. Landing tugged at his suit jacket and ushered an elegantly dressed woman toward the grand staircase.

"It's Margaret Chanler," someone whispered, an unmistakable awe in their tone.

Miss Chanler, great-granddaughter of John Jacob Astor, was well known for her philanthropic efforts despite being around Ivy's age.

But what was an Astor doing at the library? In the year since Ivy had worked there, she had rarely seen their benefactors set foot in the building. Although the Astors were rumored to favor merging the library with the Lenox Library to create a public facility, their personal involvement seemed distant at best.

As Ivy considered this unexpected visit, the sharp click of heels echoed up the staircase. She rushed back to her station at the rare books desk but could still see the stairs from her seat.

Miss Chanler emerged on the second-floor landing, a picture

of elegance in a light grey gown of fine cheviot, tailored with gigot sleeves, white silk cuffs, and a neck ruff of black net trimmed with white lace. Her poised bearing exuded the authority of her famous name.

Mr. Landing escorted the visitor directly to the librarian's desk.

Were they coming to see her? Ivy rose to her feet, clasping her hands nervously in front of her.

"Miss King, this is Miss Chanler," Mr. Landing said. "She's here to speak with you."

Ivy forced a smile. Had she done something wrong? "Good day, Miss Chanler. It's a pleasure to meet you. How may I assist you?"

The young woman extended her hand, which Ivy shook tentatively. "Actually, Miss King, I'm here to thank you for the help you've already provided to our beloved library," she said warmly. "Because of your efforts, we've stopped a villain from stealing more of our precious books, dismantled a prolific ring of thieves, and even recovered several missing volumes. The Astor Library owes you a debt of gratitude."

Relief that she wasn't losing her job flooded Ivy. "Thank you, but I didn't do much. Mr. William Walraven was the one who caught McGill."

"I've spoken to him, and he said quite emphatically that you deserved the praise." Miss Chanler smiled, handing Ivy an envelope. "I didn't want to just thank you in passing. I'll leave you to your work now, but please accept this as a token of our gratitude."

With a gracious nod, she turned away. Mr. Landing showed her around the floor briefly before they descended the stairs. The library gradually returned to its usual hush, though Ivy wasn't afforded the same peace.

A cluster of librarians swarmed her desk, eyes bright with curiosity. Ivy held the packet tightly, reluctant to open it in front of an audience. Their questions came in rapid-fire succession, but she could only manage a distracted smile as her mind replayed the encounter.

"What did she give you?" one woman asked, curiosity sparkling in her eyes.

"I don't know." With trembling hands, Ivy opened the envelope and pulled out a check from the Astor family—not a fortune, but more money than the bookstore made in a month. It was like a gift from Heaven dropped into her lap.

For the rest of the day, whispers of Ivy's unexpected recognition spread through the library like wildfire. The attention was nerve-wracking, and by the end of her shift, she was more than ready to go home. Instead, however, Mr. Landing's secretary asked her to come to the head librarian's office. Maybe he expected her to return the reward.

"Come in, Miss King," he said after she rapped on his door. "And close the door, please." He motioned for her to take the seat across from him. "We are all very proud of your diligence in keeping our collections secure. However, even before this incident, I'd noted your hard work and expertise. Now that we are without an assistant librarian, I'd like to offer you the position."

Ivy's mouth almost dropped open. A woman in that position was unheard of. "I'm honored. I assume this means full-time hours."

"It does. I know you only wanted part-time, but the pay increase would be substantial."

Her head spun with the decisions she must make. "May I have a few days to think about it? I'd like to talk with my grandmother."

"Of course, of course." Mr. Landing stood and escorted her to the door. "How about you give me your answer by Friday?"

Ivy nodded and left the office. She moved in a daze as she gathered her reticule and made her way home. Her mind whirled at all the things she needed to consider.

For the Astors, the reward might have been a mere drop in the bucket, but for the Kings, it meant they might be able to invest in the beginnings of a rare book section. If she took the full-time job, they'd be able to weather the storm a bit better when the rent increased.

But it would mean they'd have to hire someone to help Gran run the shop because Ivy would never let her grandmother handle it all on her own. And there would be no time to make a successful go at the rare book trade.

Her heart twisted in a complicated knot. Truth be told, she didn't want to be an assistant librarian. If Gran's and her financial situation weren't precarious, she'd turn the position down.

When Ivy pushed open the bookshop door, she found Gran grinning and fairly bouncing on her toes as she wrapped a customer's purchase. If she was in a good mood now, Ivy couldn't wait to see what Gran would do when she heard the news. She might even do one of those lively reels from her youth.

Once the store was empty of customers, Ivy turned to her grandmother and asked, "What's going on? You look like the cat who ate the canary."

Gran pulled Ivy into a tight embrace. "I have the most wonderful news." She twirled Ivy around the room in a dance. "We received a notice from the landlord that the rent increase has been postponed."

Ivy gasped, out of breath from the dance and the announcement. "Postponed? I've never heard of such a thing."

"Neither have I. But we're not the only ones who received a reprieve. Several businesses along the street, which were also expecting their rent to go up this month, were told the same thing. We must have a guardian angel out there somewhere."

Ivy suspected that their guardian angel had chestnut hair and hazel eyes. Had he coerced the landlord into backing down? To be sure, the threatened rent increase was egregious. As Will had told her, Denwall's power, if used appropriately, could do good.

"Did the notice say how long the increase has been postponed for?" Ivy asked.

"It appears for at least another year."

"I can't believe this." Ivy grinned and moved to the counter. "I have wonderful news as well."

"Is it better than mine?" Gran winked.

Quickly pulling the bank check from her reticule and handing it to Gran, Ivy's words came out in a rush. "The Astors gave me a reward for helping catch that book thief." She grabbed Gran's hands, and the paper drifted to the floor. "Isn't it amazing? What luck!"

"No, not luck. Blessings. The Lord has given us many blessings this day."

Indeed, He had. *God is so good.*

Maybe she wouldn't have to take the full-time job at the Astor after all. With the reprieve from the rent increase, she could use the reward money to buy a few rare books. Make a name for herself in the trade, and then maybe she and Gran would be allowed in auctions and sales. Build up a steady client list as her parents had.

Besides her bad leg, only one thing prevented Ivy from leaping joyfully.

Her time with Will was running out, and he'd not said a word about a future together.

TWENTY-SEVEN

Will strode into the foyer of his parents' Philadelphia town house.

He hadn't planned on spending the weekend in Pennsylvania. Unfortunately, he had to make the trip to handle damage control after the newspapers ran a lengthy article regarding Bert's mugging, the book thefts, and a heroine who'd not only brought down several criminals but who, as the article said, *captured the heart of William Walraven, of the Denwall dynasty.*

The reporter had no difficulty finding witnesses to corroborate all his claims. From the hospital nurses to the nosy neighbors on Ivy's street, plenty of people saw them together.

To be sure, the report was accurate. Ivy *had* captured his heart. He only wished he could have broken the news to his family before it hit the society pages.

"Thank you," Will said as he handed his hat to the butler. "Where is everybody?"

"Mrs. Walraven is in the garden with Miss Caroline. I believe Master Ned is in the drawing room."

"I'll go say hello to Ned. Would you let my mother know I'll join her shortly?"

"Certainly, sir."

In long strides, Will took the wide hall to the expansive room overlooking Rittenhouse Square. Ned lay sprawled on one of the settees, his back to the door and reading a book.

"Hello there, little brother." Will wrapped an arm around his brother's neck and rubbed his knuckles in his thick chestnut hair.

"Ow. That hurts." Ned laughed. "Let go."

Will complied, but not before tweaking Ned's ear for good measure.

"Why aren't you outside with Mother?"

Ned swung his legs around to a sitting position and ran a hand through his hair. "I needed some space from Caroline. Her chatter gets on my nerves. They should be back any minute."

"How do you know that?"

"Because Caro's chatter will begin to get on Mother's nerves as well."

Will smiled and walked to the large window. Outside, the oaks were beginning to change color. "How's school?" he asked without turning around.

"I don't know. It's just started."

"No idea whether you'll like it? Do you have Professor Ames for economics?"

"Yeah. I can't stand business classes."

Will turned from the window and took in his brother's defeated posture. "What's wrong with business classes? Bert and I took them."

"That's just it. I don't want to do what you two did."

"What do you want, then?"

"I think I'd like to study architecture."

That was the first Will had heard of it. Father would be furious.

Footsteps sounded in the hall outside the drawing room. Mother glided over the threshold, followed closely by Caroline.

"Will, I didn't know you were coming home. It's good to see you."

He bent to accept his mother's warm hug and turned to kiss his sister on the cheek. "Caro, I think you've grown since I last saw you."

Caroline frowned. "Oh dear, I hope not. I'm tall enough as it is."

"Don't worry her so, Will," Mother said. "She's almost eighteen and has certainly stopped growing."

Will chuckled. Women were so funny about their height. "Where's Father?"

"He went into the office early this morning." Mother waved a hand, as if it was of no consequence that her husband was working on a Saturday—working at all, really. But Will could see the worry in her eyes. Obviously, Father had yet to follow the doctor's orders of more time away from Denwall.

Caroline grabbed Will's arm. "You'll never guess my news."

Ned moaned. "Must we hear this again?"

Will shot his brother a quelling look. "Let's see," he said. He pursed his lips and looked at the ceiling, while Caroline bounced beside him. He snapped his fingers. "I've got it! You're marrying a prince."

Caroline's eyes twinkled. "I wish. But my news is almost as good." She paused for effect and then blurted, "Mother is letting me attend the grand opening in New York. We're coming out a few days early with the Dennisons." She held her clasped hands to her chest and bounced on her toes. "I'm so excited!"

"I can see that." It pleased Will that someone was looking forward to that day. "Are all the Dennisons coming?"

"Every single one." Mother took a seat on the settee Ned had vacated. "Myra is so excited to show those four girls in New York society, you'd think she'd given birth to them all."

Will slung an arm around Caroline's shoulders. "Thank goodness there aren't three more of you in *our* family."

She rewarded him with an elbow to his gut.

Mother turned her hazel eyes on Ned. "Why don't you and your sister go out for an ice cream?"

Ned snorted. "Out for an ice cream. What are we? Twelve?"

"I'd like to talk to William. Alone."

"Uh oh," Ned smirked at Will. "Someone's in trouble," he said in the singsong voice of a twelve-year-old.

Mother shot Ned a warning look. "I haven't seen him since he took this assignment. I'd like to catch up without prying ears."

Caroline gave Ned a shove toward the door. "We know when we're not wanted."

Will folded into a stiff-backed armchair. No sense being comfortable when he was about to get a lecture.

"Your father's secretary has been working with Holland House on the Grand Opening Ball. I think it's going to be lovely."

So, Mother wanted to chat first. Better to lull him into a sense of security then go for the jugular.

"I'm just glad it's one less thing Bert or I have to manage." Mother probably had a guiding hand in the ball's arrangements. She was a force of nature when it came to event planning.

Mother leaned forward. "You'll never guess what's happened."

"Oh, what's that?" Will wasn't expecting to spend this time gossiping, but he'd take the bait.

"Elizabeth Blake and her mother have returned from England."

He couldn't have been more surprised if she'd said the Morgans lost all their money. "What happened to the British noble?"

"I'm not entirely sure," she shrugged, "but Mrs. Blake says Elizabeth changed her mind." She sent Will a pointed look. "She hopes that you two can reconcile. Elizabeth is sorry for what happened."

He didn't believe for a second that Elizabeth had a change of heart about becoming the wife of Lord Cumbria. Something else must have happened. Like she discovered his attraction to opera singers. "No matter how contrite Elizabeth Blake is, and even if I could see past the embarrassment of being jilted, I'm not interested in a reconciliation."

"You've always talked about the perfect woman for you. Let me see if I remember correctly." His mother tapped a long finger against her chin. "Tall, blonde, smart but not too smart, and a woman of society. Good-looking, but not necessarily a beauty. Elizabeth fits the bill perfectly. Too bad she's a cold fish."

Will choked back a laugh. He hadn't realized she didn't like Elizabeth.

"There are plenty of young women in Philadelphia who meet your criteria, however."

"Ah, I see where you're headed with this." Will took his mother's hand. He needed to nip this in the bud, and the best way to do that was to tell her the truth. "There's a problem with this scheme of yours, however. It seems I've fallen in love with someone already."

Mother's mouth dropped open, but she recovered quickly and clapped her hands in delight. "Oh, Will, that's wonderful! Who is she?"

"Her name is Ivy King."

"Oh, dear." Her lips turned down. "The woman you've been seen around New York with. The bookshop owner?"

"You read the article, I take it?"

Mother placed a hand over her heart. "To read about Bert's mugging in black and white, even though he'd told us what happened, I almost fainted." Her eyes narrowed on Will's face. "Lucky for you, Bert explained why you didn't notify your father and me immediately."

He didn't regret that decision. "What did Bert tell you about Miss King?"

"Just that he liked her tremendously. But he didn't tell me you had feelings for her." She tilted her head. "So, there's no chance with Elizabeth?"

"Even if nothing comes of my relationship with Miss King, I'd never marry Elizabeth. I don't love her."

"Well, it seems God turned your idea of the perfect life on its ear."

Will chuckled. "That's one way to look at it."

"Your father will be deeply disappointed that you're not to marry Elizabeth. He's invited the Blakes to your grand opening."

Will groaned.

"He'd always hoped for a union of our two families." Mother's placating tone didn't lessen the audacity of Father to go behind Will's back.

"When I marry, it won't be to unite two families at Father's whim."

"Good for you."

Will searched his mother's face. He could tell she meant what she said. One thing about Laura Walraven—sometimes she surprised the socks off him.

"Tell me about her," she said.

And for the next twenty minutes, he did just that.

─────

After almost thirty-two years of marriage, Laura Walraven knew how to deal with her hard-headed husband, and right now she needed to prepare him for the fact that their son was in love with a bookseller from New York.

The moon cast a glow on her bedroom floor. She could hear Charles moving about in the room next to hers as he readied himself for bed. Once again, he'd missed a family dinner. In fact, by the time Charles had made it home from the office, Will had returned to his own house.

To be sure, she was grateful for her husband's success. Her life had been blessed with more abundance than she ever wanted or needed. That success, however, had come at a price. The family gatherings Charles missed. The long stretches away from home on business travel. And now, issues with his health.

Taking a deep breath, Laura laid her brush on her dressing table, smoothed the front of her dressing gown, and walked to the door separating her bedroom from her husband's. She knocked gently and then entered.

Charles sat in a leather armchair by the fireplace, a glass of brandy in his hand. Sometimes it was the only way he could sleep. "Laura, darling," he said, setting down the glass. "To what do I owe this pleasure?"

She appreciated the warmth in his eyes that had never dimmed, even after all these years. "Charles, we need to talk."

He held out a hand, and when she took it, he pulled her to his lap. "What's wrong?" Despite his faults, she never doubted his love for her.

She shifted so that she could see his face. "It's about Will."

His eyes narrowed. "Is he in trouble again?"

Letting out a frustrated sigh, she shook her head. "That was eight years ago. And it's nothing like that. But it is important. He's fallen in love."

"Well, that's wonderful news. I'm glad to hear he and Elizabeth are back together."

"It's not Miss Blake." Laura placed a hand on his chest. "Her name is Ivy King."

His smile vanished, and his jaw tightened. "The bookseller? The woman the news reports said people have seen him with?"

"Yes," Laura replied, keeping her tone calm and steady. "Will told me about her today. She sounds lovely."

"A bookseller," Charles repeated, his voice hardening. "I always thought he would marry someone from our circle. A bookseller is hardly suitable for a Walraven."

Her patience waning, she slid off his lap to stand before him, hands on her hips. "And what exactly is *suitable*, Charles?

Someone with money and connections but no substance? He's found someone he loves, someone who makes him happy. It's what I've always wanted for him."

Charles pushed himself from the chair and began pacing the room. "You know the expectations placed on him. On all of us. Marrying beneath his station will reflect poorly on the entire family."

"And those expectations have often been a burden," she countered, her voice rising. "We've seen what happens when people marry for convenience rather than love. I don't want that for Will. For any of our children."

Charles stopped, turning to face her. "It's not just about love. It's about maintaining our family's reputation, our standing in society. A bookseller can't possibly understand our world."

"From what Will tells me, she understands *him*," Laura shot back. "And she understands the value of hard work, of integrity. Those are qualities that matter far more than social standing."

"This is not a matter for debate. William has responsibilities. He cannot simply follow his heart without considering the consequences."

Her temper flared. "And what about the consequences of denying him his happiness? Have you considered that? Or are you so blinded by pride that you can't see what's best for our son?"

The room crackled with tension. "You speak of pride, but you fail to see the bigger picture. This marriage could ruin everything we've built."

"Or it could enrich it," Laura said, her voice trembling with emotion. "If we give Miss King a chance, we might find she brings out the best in Will. She could be a wonderful addition to our family."

"You're asking too much." His face reddened as it always did when he was angry. Yet now she had to worry that his emotions would cause a setback in his health.

"I'm asking for an open mind. For our son's sake." She softened her tone. "We'll talk about this later. I just needed you to know what was going on." She handed him the brandy he'd set on the table. "Here. Hopefully it will calm your nerves."

She let out a frustrated breath. Her announcement had gone much worse than she feared.

But, for Will's sake, she wasn't about to back down.

TWENTY-EIGHT

Will's heart pounded with pride and trepidation as he stood at the entrance of Denwall, ready to welcome the eager crowd gathered outside. Every detail, every bit of work over the past three months, had led to this moment.

"Are you ready?" Bert asked, giving Will a reassuring sideways glance. "You know everything's going to be fine, right?"

Not entirely confident, Will nodded anyway. "Where's Father?" he asked, scanning the crowd.

Bert pointed toward the second-floor balcony. Charles Walraven surveyed the scene from above, hands clasped behind his back like a captain commanding his ship. The sight made Will's palms sweat, and he glanced at his watch. Time to discover whether their hard work would pay off.

With a signal to the doormen, the enormous brass doors swung open, and the crowd of shoppers poured through the entryway. Some moved with purposeful steps, while others strolled in, taking in their surroundings with awe. To add a personal touch, Will greeted as many visitors as possible.

His mother glided in when the initial rush slowed, with Ned and Caroline trailing behind. "I want to experience the store like a shopper," she said, glancing up at her husband, who still held his command spot on the second floor, "not like an owner."

"Since you want the shopper's experience, please make sure you buy something, Mother." Will bumped Ned with his shoulder. "You, too, little brother."

Ned shrugged, hands in his pockets, fully aware how his nonchalance regarding anything Denwall irritated his family.

Caroline lifted her reticule. "I've been saving my pin money, Will."

Will slipped an arm around his pretty sister's shoulders. "I knew I could count on you."

"Have you seen the Dennisons?" Mother asked.

"James is around somewhere, but I haven't seen Myra or the others yet."

"Myra's probably calculated the most opportune time to make her entrance."

A force to be reckoned with, Myra Dennison had an uncanny knack for great timing. But Will wasn't interested in Myra or any of James's five offspring. He waited for Ivy. At some point in the past few weeks, her good opinion had become more important than even his father's.

Bert had been checking on the progress of various departments and returned to the main floor in time to escort Caroline around to spend her money, and Ned wandered off to find something to eat.

Mother stuck to Will's side like glue. What was she up to?

"Has Ivy arrived yet?" she asked.

And there was his answer. His nosy mother was hoping to meet the woman who'd captured his heart. "I haven't seen her. But she'll be here."

Sage, the reporter from *The Daily New Yorker,* appeared at Will's side. "Would you be willing to give me an interview later, Mr. Walraven?"

"Certainly. Browse the store, and we'll meet in two hours. You can come upstairs to my office. Does that work for you?"

"It does. I'll see you then."

Will shook the man's hand.

When the reporter moved out of sight, the bustling store faded to silence, and time seemed to stop. Ivy, accompanied by her aunt and grandmother, stepped across the entryway threshold. Will stood rooted in his spot, struck by how much this moment mattered. He sent up a silent prayer that she'd like the store.

Her blue eyes met his gaze, and her lips curved into a warm smile. She waved, and he moved toward her.

"Welcome to Denwall," he said when he reached her side. "Thank you all for coming." Their support meant the world to him.

Ivy held out her hand, and he grasped it. "This is amazing, Will. Beyond what I imagined."

"I think I'll just wander around," Mrs. Capp said. "Jemima, would you like to join me?"

Mrs. King grinned. "Why, certainly." She winked at him.

Will pulled Ivy's hand through the crook in his elbow. "My mother wants to meet you, and then I'll take you on a tour." Will hoped she wouldn't mind meeting his family.

"I'd love to do both." She squeezed his arm.

Mother met them halfway and enveloped Ivy in a hug. "I've heard so much about you, my dear."

Ivy smiled shyly. "And I, you."

"You're a brave young woman. My sons are blessed to know you." Mother leaned back, still holding Ivy's shoulders. "I'm so glad you're coming to the ball tonight. You'll be a breath of fresh air in a room full of puffed-up peacocks."

Ivy's blue eyes turned to liquid pools, and Will handed her a handkerchief.

"Mother, you've made her cry, and it only took you ten seconds. I think that's a record."

Ivy understood the lure of the department store. Row upon row of merchandise, from exquisite gowns to fine jewelry, pulled the customer in. The air was filled with the scent of new leather, perfumes, and the hushed excitement of shoppers. As they strolled through the store, she couldn't help but feel a sense of wonder at the sheer scale of Denwall. Her fingers trailed over delicate fabrics and well-crafted leather.

With her arm wrapped in his, Ivy couldn't miss the tension in Will's tight muscles. This grand opening was a significant moment —a chance to prove himself to his father and earn the coveted position of head of the company.

Will led her around, showing her the different departments that set Denwall apart. Ivy's gaze traveled over rows of men's coats, from all-wool cheviots priced at six dollars to sumptuous velvet-piped coats at forty-five dollars. Shoes lined the walls, each pair gleaming under the soft lighting.

"Each department aims to quickly turn over merchandise as needed. As we head into the cold weather, our customers need warm coats, hence our featured item."

Logical. Department stores couldn't hang on to last season's clothes for too long without suffering slumping sales. How difficult it must be to keep abreast of the latest trends.

"So I assume you have experienced buyers who understand the customer's needs."

"Right, and who can predict the coming trends as well." Will tipped his head toward the elevator. "Let's go up to the fifth floor." His voice dropped to almost a whisper. "I have so much to talk to you about." His eyes searched her upturned face, and his voice was serious, yet warm.

A touch of hope dared to spark. Did he want a future with her?

They followed several shoppers onto the elegant elevator. After stopping at each floor, the bell dinged and the doors opened on the fifth floor.

The stationery and book department reminded her of a smaller version of the Charles Scribner store—neat and orderly but lacking the cozy charm of her own shop. However, signs boasted much lower prices than the King bookstore could offer.

Will cleared his throat. "As you can see, the space is less inviting than your bookshop. We can't carry specialty items like you do. Having my staff hunt down rare books and determine their worth wastes manpower." He hesitated and drew a deep breath. "What if we combined forces?"

Not the most romantic of proposals. Ivy chewed her bottom lip. "What do you mean?"

"I know you'd like to sell rare books and that new releases are less lucrative, what with publishers cutting booksellers' slice of the profit. Let Denwall focus on the new book market, where we have the advantage of size and clout, and the King bookshop will become a center for rare books." When she couldn't find her voice to respond, he rushed on, "I'd provide the capital to get you started, and make sure you had an agent to escort you to auctions."

He looked so pleased with his idea. How could she tell him her heart was breaking?

She cleared her constricting throat. "I appreciate such a generous offer. Let me think about it." The last thing she wanted was to feel like Will's charity project.

"Of course. I wouldn't expect anything less from an astute businesswoman."

Was that all he had to say?

Will guided Ivy toward the elevator. "I think I still need to show you the hats on the third floor."

"A man who knows what a woman wants to hear." She'd never admit what she'd really desired. It would be embarrassing for both of them. Focused on steadying her breathing, she tried not to cry.

In the millinery department, sunlight streamed through tall windows, catching the shimmer of feathers and silk ribbons atop hats perched delicately on display stands. The department hummed with activity as shopgirls helped customers try on the latest styles in front of strategically placed mirrors.

Will moved back to allow Ivy a better view. "And here we have—"

A sudden, distinct pop came from under her skirt. The platform shoe wobbled, and her heart drummed in her ears. She put a hand on Will's arm to steady herself and hoisted her foot to assess the damage. With one last pop, the entire platform detached from the leather sole, clattering to the polished floor like a discarded biscuit tin lid.

Ivy's stomach plummeted as heads turned. A young boy pointed at her shoe with wide-eyed curiosity until his mother tugged him away.

"Ivy—" Will's voice was soft, concerned, but her face burned too brightly to meet his gaze.

"It's fine," she said quickly, fumbling to retrieve the rogue platform. Clutching the piece of her shoe like some absurd trophy, she forced a laugh. "Happens sometimes."

Will dipped his head so he could look her in the face. "You're not hurt, are you?"

"Only my pride," she muttered, wishing the ground would swallow her whole.

"I'd be happy to carry you." His lopsided grin almost made her forget the mortifying situation.

"I can manage, thanks."

The thudding of her uneven gait drew more unwanted attention with every step.

"Sit over there and give me your shoe," he said, pointing to a vacant chair. "I'll take it to the cobbler we have on staff. We'll have it fixed in no time."

Ivy exhaled, her shoulders sinking as he guided her to the chair.

When he walked away, she turned to find a tall man staring at her, hands behind his back like he was the captain of a ship. His mouth turned down in a frown.

"Mr. Walraven," one of the salesmen said to the man, "may I help you, sir?"

Will's father. No wonder he looked at her with disgust.

What would he think when she showed up at the ball tonight?

Ivy's insides quivered, and she worried she might cast up her accounts on Denwall's newly polished marble floor.

TWENTY-NINE

Will patted the jacket pocket holding a black velvet jeweler's box and stepped into the ballroom. The guests at the Denwall ball were varied, from family and friends arriving from Philadelphia to members of New York's Four Hundred. Political dignitaries and even the police chief had accepted the invitation to attend.

Despite the sea of well-to-do people he needed to greet, shake hands with, and thank, there was only one person he sought. Her visit to Denwall earlier that day had left him jittery. Ivy hadn't reacted the way he hoped she would at his proposition to combine bookselling efforts.

Thinking about it later, he almost kicked himself. Hard. He sent up a silent prayer that he'd handle his marriage proposal with more aplomb.

Bert stood to the side of the ballroom, tugging at his tie, and Will strode over to give his brother a hearty slap on the back.

"It's warm in here, don't you think?" Bert grumbled.

"It's fine. Are you nervous, big brother?"

"Why on earth would I be nervous? We're at a ball with people I've known all my life who, despite knowing I can't stand dancing, will expect me to anyway. And then there's the large contingent of New York's Four Hundred, who look like they're searching for fresh prey to pounce on." Bert pushed his spectacles up his nose. "I repeat, why on earth should I be nervous?"

Will placed a reassuring hand on Bert's shoulder. "Hang in there. The whole affair will be over before you know it, and soon, you'll be returning to your cozy house on Locust Street."

"I can't wait."

Will's eyes roamed the room and locked on a group of people he'd hoped wouldn't attend the festivities. He hadn't seen the Blakes at the grand opening, so he assumed they'd decided not to make the trip to New York.

No such luck.

"Will, there you are." Mrs. Blake glided over, Elizabeth trailing behind.

Will took the older woman's hand. "Good evening, Mrs. Blake." He gave Elizabeth a polite smile. "I hope you are enjoying your stay in New York."

"We are, indeed." Mrs. Blake moved to Bert's side and pulled his arm. "Robert, will you be so kind as to escort me to find my husband?"

Bert blinked. "Um, certainly."

Elizabeth sneaked a hand through Will's arm. "I'm parched. Let's go find some refreshment."

Will's jaw ticked at the idea of being railroaded. But what else could he do but go along with her? He couldn't openly rebuff a Blake.

She tugged Will closer and gazed up at him, her eyelashes batting coquettishly. "Come, now, Will. You're so distant."

Will stopped just short of a smirk. He pulled her to the corner of the ballroom where they'd be out of the earshot of nosy guests. "After the trick you pulled in May, you expect me to be warm and cuddly?"

Her eyes filled with tears, and they didn't seem fake. "Please, don't be upset with me. I thought I was in love." She sounded more sincere than he'd ever heard her.

He understood how Elizabeth must have felt. That earth-moving sensation of finding the person you believe you are meant to be with.

He blew out a breath. "What happened?"

"I discovered he didn't care for anything but my money, so I returned his ring."

"I'm sorry, Elizabeth." And he was. To find out that the one you were in love with only wanted you for financial reasons must cut deeply.

"I decided then and there that what you and I had was a better way to enter marriage—with friendship, respect, and commonality. It's what our fathers want. Can we try again?"

"I am truly sorry. But now I've found love and can't settle for anything less."

"That shopgirl?" She spat out the words.

His back stiffened. "Miss King is a lovely woman. Beautiful. Smart. And honorable."

"Your father will never approve." Elizabeth's green eyes hardened like jade. "Mark my words, you'll regret it if you decide to build a life with someone so obviously out of our social circle. You'll be ostracized and ridiculed."

"I'm willing to risk it."

<hr/>

Ivy's heart pounded as she took in the grandeur of the ballroom. The delicate green décor, the ceiling panels depicting classically draped dancing women, and the luminaries that graced the room created an ambiance of elegance.

Gilded chairs in white upholstery provided seating for the large number of guests—over three hundred if she had to guess. With their sweeping brass arms, graceful chandeliers bathed the room in a soft, warm light, casting a romantic glow over the crystal-adorned tables. Couples twirled around the gleaming parquet floor, adding to the enchanting scene.

She wished Gran had agreed to come with her and Zella. She would have loved this. Instead, she said she was too old for such frivolity and would prefer to keep Dickens and a good book company.

Zella touched Ivy's arm. "Are you ready?"

"As ready as I'll ever be." Ivy couldn't help but feel a sense of awe as she looked around, her heart thudding with the realization that she was like a fish out of water, immersed in a glamorous world far from her humble bookstore.

Nevertheless, she promised to do herself, her family, and her neighborhood proud.

Zella picked up her skirts and glided down the stairs. Of course, Ivy didn't glide so much as carefully negotiate each step, her movements deliberate and measured, mindful of her shorter leg. She held the banister with one hand, her free hand clutching her skirts, and her head held high.

As they moved farther into the ballroom, Ivy spotted Will, so handsome in black and white evening clothes. Next to him was a beautiful woman, tall and elegant, with blonde tresses pulled up in a fashionable hairdo. When someone called out, "Miss Blake," the woman turned.

Ivy's short-lived confidence crumbled to dust. This must be Elizabeth, the woman who left Will for a peer of the British realm. Considering how she'd been cozying up to Will just seconds before, she must be still unmarried. *Would his interest in her rekindle?*

The elegant woman walked away, leaving Will standing alone. His gaze met Ivy's, and the warmth in his eyes made her heart sing. He walked toward her, his steps confident and purposeful.

"You look stunning," he murmured as he reached for her hand, his eyes filled with adoration.

"You clean up rather nicely yourself." Although she'd argued with Zella about wearing such a fancy gown, she thanked the Lord for her stubborn aunt. And for Will's thoughtfulness at sending her a pair of lovely shoes he'd had made by his cobbler. At least they wouldn't come apart on her, as her boot had so embarrassingly done earlier in the day.

"Can I get you something to drink?" he asked.

"No, thank you. I'm fine right now."

She searched the ballroom for a sign of Will's father. He must be here somewhere and would most likely know she was on the guest list. Would his eyes hold the disdain she'd seen at the store opening?

Will tucked her hand in his and signaled to the orchestra. Soon, the strains of a waltz filled the ballroom. "May I have the first dance?"

She glanced at the couples making their way onto the dance floor. Her nerves jittered, but she summoned a smile. Could she get through the next few minutes without making a fool of herself for Will's sake?

"Of course," she said after a moment's hesitation.

Please, Lord, guide my steps.

She needn't have worried.

Will enveloped her left hand in his right, and she rested her other hand lightly on his upper arm. His hand on her waist was both firm and gentle, the heat of his touch seeping through layers of satin and lace, sending a delightful shiver through her. Expertly guiding her through a sea of swirling gowns and tailored evening suits, his eyes remained on her face, and she couldn't look away.

When the dance finished, Will walked her around the room and toward a conservatory at the far west side of the ballroom. The glass-enclosed space was a haven of peace away from the music and chatter, filled with potted palms and the sweet scent of night-blooming jasmine. Moonlight filtered through the glass ceiling, casting silver shadows that danced among the foliage.

He turned to face her, his expression suddenly serious yet tender. His hands trembled slightly as he reached for hers, and Ivy's heart began to race. She knew, somehow, that this moment would change everything.

"Ivy," he began, his voice thick with emotion, "from the first day you walked into my life, everything changed. Your quick wit and gentle heart brought light and laughter into my world. I love your courage and your strength of character."

He slipped his hand into his pocket and pulled out a black velvet box. Her heart tripped, and her hand flew to her mouth. When he sank to one knee on the conservatory's marble floor, tears welled in her eyes.

He opened the box to reveal a gleaming diamond ring, its facets catching the moonlight and throwing tiny rainbows across her dress. "Ivy King, you've shown me what true love really means. It's not about social standing or family expectations—it's about finding someone who makes you want to be better, someone who understands you completely and loves you anyway. I don't know what the future holds, but I know that every day with you is a gift I want to treasure forever. Will you do me the extraordinary honor of becoming my wife?"

Her eyes filled, her vision blurred, and her throat closed, but she managed to nod. This was better than any dream she could have conjured.

With deft fingers, he pulled off her glove and put the band on her finger. It was a perfect fit, as if it had been waiting for this moment all along. She still couldn't find her voice, so she just nodded again, tears of joy streaming down her cheeks.

Will put his arms around her waist, lifting her off the ground. "You've made me the happiest man in New York. Probably the world." He gently set her down, pressing his forehead against hers. Her heart soared at the intimate gesture.

Reality intruded on the blissful moment, however, and Ivy bit her lip. "What about your family? I'm not sure they're going to like us getting married."

"Leave my family to me. I'll tell them later. For now, let's just enjoy the ball." He brushed away a tear from her cheek with his thumb, and in his eyes she saw all the love and certainty she needed.

Wanting to catch her breath and check that her eyes didn't look too puffy from crying before she returned to the ballroom, Ivy excused herself and headed to the ladies' room. Thankful that the place was empty, she ran her handkerchief under running water and slid into one of the chairs to check her face in a mirror. Although her eyes didn't look too bad, she dabbed the cool cloth underneath them, taking a moment to savor the silence.

The door opened, and someone took the seat beside her. Ivy opened her eyes and glanced to her left to find the last person she wanted to encounter—Elizabeth Blake.

Should she just ignore her? Did one have to strike up a conversation in a ladies' room?

"I know you think that because you've connived an offer from William that your life will be wonderful." Elizabeth's voice dripped with sarcasm.

Ivy pushed back her chair, grabbed her reticule, and skirted Elizabeth's chair.

"I'm not finished." The woman rose and gripped Ivy's forearm. "Have you considered what your life will be like as a Walraven? You've only gotten a taste of what it's like to be scrutinized by the public. They're being nice to you now because they've made you into some kind of heroine. But mark my words, they'll turn on you. The well-to-do don't take kindly to interlopers. The society columns will remark on every event you attend. Every dress you wear." Her green eyes took in Ivy's gown and then her new shoes. "Believe me when I tell you that even your hideous shoes will be scrutinized."

I don't have to listen to this. "If you'll excuse me." Ivy narrowed her eyes on the hand that remained on her arm.

Stepping back, Elizabeth said, "I'm telling you this for your own good. For Will's own good. Do you think he, or his family, will welcome the public ridicule they'll undoubtedly receive?"

Refusing to let the hateful woman see her cry, Ivy turned toward the exit, though she didn't have the heart to return to the ballroom.

But she wasn't a quitter. She'd see this night through with her head held high. Even though a voice inside her head told her Elizabeth was right. *How will I ever fit into Will's world?*

THIRTY

Sunday morning sunlight streamed through the bookshop window, catching dust motes that danced in the air as Ivy ran her cleaning cloth over the counter. Her engagement ring caught the light and twinkled.

Last night's events floated in her head like a dream—the grand ballroom, the romantic proposal, Will's loving words. But in the stark morning light, doubt stuck in her head like a sharp hatpin.

Her gaze drifted to the newspaper she'd been reading earlier, with its glowing descriptions of last night's ball. There, in a corner, was a depiction of Elizabeth Blake, looking every inch the society beauty. Ivy's stomach churned. Elizabeth would know how to manage a grand house, how to host the elaborate parties expected of a Walraven wife, how to navigate the treacherous waters of the upper crust.

Her hand stilled on the counter as her mind raced. Where would they live? Philadelphia was out of the question—she couldn't leave New York or Gran. She couldn't abandon the book-shop. It was more than just a business. It was her heritage, her parents' legacy, her very identity. The thought of walking away from it made her want to weep.

She absently massaged her aching hip and peered down at her ugly platformed shoe. Will might see past it, might truly not care, but Philadelphia society wouldn't be so kind. They would whisper behind their fans, make cutting remarks about the lame shopgirl who'd somehow snared the second oldest Walraven.

A sharp rap at the window startled her from her thoughts. Her heart pounded, and she moved to unlock the door, even though she'd like nothing better than to pretend she didn't know Charles Walraven stood on the other side.

"Miss King." His voice was clipped, formal, and as cold as a January wind.

"Good morning, Mr. Walraven," she managed, her fingers twisting together. "Will isn't here—"

"I know where my son is. This won't take long." He removed his hat but didn't unbutton his coat. His face was flushed, whether from the cold or anger, she couldn't tell. "I understand William proposed to you last night."

"Yes, he did." She lifted her chin slightly, trying to project a confidence she didn't feel.

"I'll be direct, Miss King. This cannot happen." His expensive boots clicked against the floor as he moved to stand directly in front of her. "You seem like a respectable young woman, and I don't doubt that you care for William. But surely you must see how impossible this is."

"Mr. Walraven, I love—"

He held up his hand, cutting her off. "Love is irrelevant. Let me lay out the facts." His face grew redder as he spoke. "You are a shopkeeper—a very good one, I'm sure—but my son will be chief executive of one of the largest emporiums in the nation." His lip curled slightly. "You could never fit into our world, Miss King. Surely you must see that."

He pressed a hand to his chest, seeming to struggle for breath for a moment before continuing, "If William goes through with this foolish notion of marriage, he will regret it for the rest of his life. More than that, he will lose his position at Denwall. I refuse to let him destroy decades of hard work and reputation for a romantic whim."

The words hit like slap to the face. Each one confirmed her own doubts, her own fears.

"Think carefully, Miss King. Are you willing to be the reason William loses everything he's worked for? Everything he was born to become?"

Without waiting for her response, he settled his hat back on his head and strode to the door. Hand on the knob, he turned and shot her a look that made her insides quiver. "I trust you'll be sensible and make the right decision." The bell above the door chimed, sounding eerily cheerful in the heavy silence he left behind.

Ivy sank onto her stool behind the counter, her legs no longer able to support her. With trembling fingers, she slipped the diamond ring from her finger and placed it on the counter. The sight of it there, catching the morning light, brought fresh tears to her eyes.

She pulled a sheet of paper from beneath the counter and picked up her pen. The words came slowly. Painfully.

Dearest Will,

I can't marry you. I would never fit into your world, and I refuse to be the reason you lose everything you've worked for. Please don't try to change my mind. This is for the best.

I'm sorry.

Ivy

She folded the note carefully and placed it with the ring. In an hour, she would have them delivered to Will's hotel. For now, she sat in the quiet of her shop, surrounded by her beloved books, and let the sobs wrack her body.

Laura descended the hotel's grand staircase and approached the front desk. Charles had crept out of their suite before she'd had her first cup of coffee.

"Have you seen my husband?" she asked the clerk.

"Mr. Walraven left about an hour ago. I haven't seen him return, but he might have come in through one of our other entrances." He turned to the rows of cubby holes behind him. "There are some messages for your family here, however."

"I'll take them," Laura said absently, her eyes searching the foyer for Charles.

The clerk handed her several calling cards and a small, brown paper-wrapped box. Probably a hostess gift from one of the ball's attendees.

"Thank you." She unwrapped the box, and she gasped at the glint of diamond that shone from within. Was this the ring Will gave to Ivy last night? Should she open the note and find out why the young woman had returned it?

Of course she should. She was Will's mother and wanted to know what he was facing.

Her heart sank when she read Ivy's words, the elegant handwriting marred by what appeared to be teardrops on the paper.

"Charles," Laura whispered, "what have you done?"

She knew her husband well enough to recognize his handiwork. How many times had she observed him steamroll people in the name of what was best for the family? But this time, he'd gone too far.

She re-wrapped the package, secured the note back in its envelope, and left it with the desk clerk. "Please have this delivered to William's room and tell him I've gone out for a while, but to wait for me before he goes anywhere."

"Of course, Mrs. Walraven. I'll deliver it personally."

Laura ordered a carriage and soon she'd arrived at the Kings' doorstep. The streets were quiet this early on a Sunday morning, but a light burned in the bookshop window.

She rapped gently on the glass. Through it, she saw a massive Saint Bernard lift its head, rise, and trot to the door. Ivy appeared from the back room, her eyes red-rimmed and her face pale.

"Mrs. Walraven." Ivy's voice was barely a whisper as she opened the door. "I, I—"

"I saw the ring and your note. May I come in?"

Ivy stepped back and lifted her chin. "I meant what I wrote. I won't ruin Will's future."

"My dear girl." Laura took Ivy's trembling hand in hers. "Whatever Charles said to you, he was wrong."

"He may have been harsh, but he wasn't completely wrong. I'm a bookseller, far beneath your station. Will lives in Philadelphia. I live here, and I don't plan on leaving my family behind or my bookstore."

"Marriage is about compromise. I know you and Will can work this out." Laura squeezed Ivy's hand. "Will has regaled me with all that you do here. He's so proud of you, and I believe you'd make a wonderful wife to him."

Fresh tears spilled down Ivy's cheeks. "I do love him. So much."

"I know you do. I believe with my whole heart that you and Will are perfect for one another."

The massive dog padded over and pressed against Ivy's skirts as if lending support. "Your husband doesn't agree. And soon the newspapers will turn on you because of me," Ivy said.

"First, Will must have told you we weren't always society darlings. There was a time when we were outsiders. Greedy merchants not fit to be in the same room as old Philadelphia society. We're used to public scrutiny." She dropped Ivy's hand and narrowed her gaze. "Second, my husband is about to learn some hard truths about what truly matters in life."

Laura changed her tone to one she'd used often on her children—one that brooked no argument. "Don't let Charles's pride steal your happiness. Or Will's. My husband has refused to enjoy the life he's been given, but instead always strives for more. But look what it's gotten him. A weak heart and a son who feels he can never measure up."

"I don't want that for Will," Ivy whispered.

"Then fight for him. For both of you." Laura stepped back. "Now, if you'll excuse me, I have a husband to set straight."

Her mind went through a dozen ways to wring her husband's neck on the return trip to Holland House. Exiting the elevator on their floor, she glimpsed Will rounding the corner and heading straight for their hotel suite door. By the set of his shoulders, he was itching for a fight.

THIRTY-ONE

Will's hands trembled with barely contained anger as he strode down the hotel's carpeted hallway. The diamond ring clutched in his palm cut into his flesh, but the physical pain was nothing compared to the ache in his heart when he'd read Ivy's note.

He struck the door of his parents' suite with enough force to make the elaborate brass numbers rattle. Father's valet opened the door.

"Where's my father?" Will demanded.

"He's in the sitting room with Mr. Dennison, sir."

Will brushed past, his footsteps heavy against the plush carpet. He found his father and James seated in leather chairs, a tray of coffee and pastries in front of them.

"What did you say to Ivy?" Will demanded without preamble, his voice filling the elegant room. "What did you do?"

His father's expression remained impassive, though a muscle twitched in his jaw. "I merely had a conversation with Miss King. One that was long overdue."

"A conversation?" Will's laugh was harsh, caustic. "You threatened her, didn't you? Bullied her until she had no choice but to return this." He held Ivy's ring in two fingers, right in front of his father's nose.

James set his cup aside and let out a loud breath while his eyes narrowed on Father's face. "Charles, what exactly did you do?"

"What needed to be done." Father's voice was firm, but he wouldn't meet James's eyes. "Someone had to make the girl see reason."

Will clenched his fists at his sides. "You know what? I've realized something. I don't *want* to step into your shoes anymore. I don't *want* to become you." Father flinched at the words, but Will pressed on, "For years, I've tried to live up to your expectations, to be the son you wanted."

Will stepped back, before he gave into the urge to take his father by the shoulders and shake him. "You've sacrificed everything for Denwall—family, relationships, even your own happiness. And you expect me to do the same."

His father surged to his feet, face flushed. "Everything I've done has been for this family!"

"No," Will cut in, his voice steady now. "Everything you've done has been for Denwall. There's a difference." He took a deep breath. "I'm done with it all. I'll make my own way, with or without your blessing."

"You'd give up Denwall for a woman?" Father sputtered.

"Not just for Ivy, though she's the kindest, smartest, most beautiful woman I've ever known. I'm doing this for myself too. I want a different life than yours. One where business success doesn't come at the cost of everything else."

James rose from his chair and shook his head. "Well, well, my friend. It's a fine pickle you've gotten yourself into."

Father's expression brightened momentarily. "I knew *you'd* understand, James. How does he think walking away from his birthright will work?"

"I wasn't referring to Will."

Father eyes grew as big as saucers. "What are you talking about?"

"You're the one in a pickle, Charles. Will's not just making a choice about love. He's making a choice about the kind of man he wants to be. And from where I'm standing, he's choosing wisely."

"But—"

Mother, who'd been uncommonly silent, stepped farther into the room. "James, make them both see reason. Surely there's a compromise here somewhere."

"I'm not about to compromise—" Father's voice rose again.

"Be quiet, Charles." James held up a hand. "Laura's right. Let's stay calm and talk this through." He glanced at Will. "William doesn't need Denwall. Any one of our competitors would jump at the chance to have him in their executive offices."

Father folded his arms across his chest. He wasn't going to give an inch.

"Denwall, however, needs Will," James continued. "He's done an outstanding job here despite the tremendous and undo pressure you put him under."

"Thank you, sir." If nothing came of James's efforts, Will would be forever grateful for the man's encouragement.

"Look, we need to hammer this out with the board, but I propose that Will stay in New York. Stay with Denwall. Our presence here is new, and we'll need his steady hand. He's already built strong business relationships in the three months he's been here." James smiled at Will. "And some personal ones as well."

"James is right. Please, don't let pride prevent you from seeing what's best for our son." Mother moved to stand directly in front of her husband. "He loves her, Charles. And she's a lovely young woman, more than deserving of him."

Father sank back, the fight seeming to drain from him. "But how can a bookseller's daughter understand our world, our responsibilities?"

Mother sat on the arm of his chair. "Maybe she'll understand better than you think. After all, she's held down two jobs and kept her business going in the face of her parents' deaths. And maybe her influence will help Will create something unique—a blend of both our worlds."

She placed her hand on Father's shoulder. "I know you're worried about the future. But you need to start trusting Will. He deserves that much for as hard as he's worked to please you." With one finger, she turned his face toward hers. "Besides, if you don't work this out, I'll never forgive you."

Father stared at her for a moment. When she didn't take back her words, he shrugged. "William's already said he doesn't want to work for Denwall, so it's a moot point." He turned and glared at Will as though every problem they had was his fault.

"I'm willing to stay on, under several conditions," Will said. Even though he prayed he could stay at Denwall's New York store, he didn't want to appear weak. "I marry who I want, and you'll be nothing but kindness and solicitude to her. And you will apologize profusely for the way I imagine you spoke to her. As far as Denwall goes, I'll not have you breathing down my neck."

Mother rose and stood beside Will. "That's not going to happen because your father is officially retiring like he promised he would. No more going into work. His health is the priority. Right, Charles?" Her voice was an effective mix of steel and honey.

Father sighed and laid his head against the back of his chair. "Fine. But quit your badgering. I have a weak heart."

Will ran a hand through his hair. He was under no delusion that Father would change overnight. But it was a start, and at least Will could be in New York rather than under Charles Walraven's nose.

He slipped Ivy's ring into his pocket, and before more arguments could break out, strode toward the door. His mother caught his arm before he crossed the threshold and pressed a quick kiss to his cheek.

"Go get her," she whispered.

Will found the bookshop's front door locked, but light spilled from the back room like a beacon guiding him home. His heart raced with hope rather than anger now—he finally had a future to offer that wouldn't force Ivy to choose between his world and hers.

Dickens, who was lying by the counter, lifted his head when Will rang the bell, and let out a low woof. His tail thumped the floor.

Ivy appeared from the back room, her eyes red and swollen from crying. She froze when she saw him, one hand flying to her throat.

"Please, Ivy," he called through the glass. "We need to talk."

She hesitated only a moment before moving to unlock the door. "Will, you shouldn't be here." Her voice was hoarse. "Your father made it very clear—"

"My father is wrong," Will interrupted, stepping inside. "And he knows it." He pulled her ring from his pocket, the diamond catching the morning light. "This belongs to you. It will always belong to you."

"You don't understand." Fresh tears spilled down her cheeks. "I can't be the reason you lose everything you've worked for. Your father was right—I'll never fit into that world."

"Then we'll create our own world." Will caught her hands in his. "Listen to me, Ivy. Everything's changed. I'll run the New York store permanently. Denwall needs me here more than in Philadelphia."

Hope flickered in her eyes before doubt clouded them again. "But what about when your father retires? Won't you need to take over in Philadelphia then?"

Will smiled, tucking a stray curl behind her ear. "Father is retiring—really retiring this time. Mother's insisting on it for his health. But someone else will need to fill his shoes. It won't be me.

I can do more good building something new here than trying to maintain the status quo in Philadelphia."

"Your father agreed to all this?" Ivy's voice was skeptical.

"He did. Though I suspect Mother's threat to never forgive him if he didn't might have helped." Will chuckled. "The point is, we don't have to choose between *my* family's business and *your* family's legacy. We can have both."

Dickens had padded over during their conversation. He pressed against Ivy's skirts, and she absently stroked his head.

"But your father still won't approve of me," she said.

"Actually, Mother made some interesting points about that too. About how you've successfully run your own business, how you understand commerce and customers in a way most society women never could." Will lifted her chin. "She thinks you'll help me create something unique here—a blend of both our worlds."

"Your mother said that?"

"She did. And Father has promised to apologize to you himself for the things he said this morning." Will's jaw tightened briefly at the memory of her tear-stained note. "Though I warn you, Charles Walraven's apologies tend to be rather gruff affairs."

A watery laugh escaped her lips. "I think I can handle gruff."

"I know you can. You're the strongest person I know." Will sank to one knee, still holding her hands in his. "Which is why I'm asking you again—Ivy King, will you marry me? Will you help me build something new here in New York, something that honors both our families' legacies while creating our own?"

Her blue eyes shimmered with fresh tears, but her smile was radiant. "Yes. Yes, to all of it."

Will placed the ring on her finger where it belonged, stood, and pulled her into his arms. She felt so right there, like she'd been made to fit against him. The familiar scent of honeysuckle filled his senses.

"I love you," he whispered against her hair. "I should have said it properly before. I love everything about you—your kindness, your strength, the way you remember every customer's name and favorite book. I love watching you with your grandmother and this overgrown puppy of yours." He reached down to scratch Dickens's ears, earning a happy whine. "I love that you'll help make Denwall's book department something special while building your own rare book collection here. I love that you'll make me a better man."

"I love you too." Ivy stretched up on her toes to kiss him properly. "But something's been bothering me."

Hadn't they had enough obstacles?

She tilted her head and gave him a mischievous smile. "Did you have something to do with my rent increase being postponed? I believe in miracles, but that one had your name written all over it."

He ducked his head and kissed the tip of her nose. "I might have had a talk with your landlord. Pointed out how businesses would look at this area for potential sites with Denwall coming in. Convinced him it wouldn't look good if the existing businesses were hit with a rent hike. But I promise I didn't bribe him."

"I never once considered you'd offered a bribe. I know the man you are, William Walraven. A man of integrity." She ran her hand up the side of his face and through his hair in a gentle caress.

He felt it all the way to his toes. "You should be aware that I'm not above bribing my wife for favors."

She giggled when he nuzzled her with his nose and then sighed when he moved his lips to run kisses up her neck and behind her ear.

Apparently deciding the reconciliation had gone on long enough, Dickens wedged himself between them with a plaintive whine.

"I think someone's ready for a walk," Ivy giggled.

"Well, then." Will offered her his arm with an exaggerated bow. "Shall we take our chaperone for a stroll? I believe we have a wedding to start planning."

She slipped her hand into the crook of his arm, and he

marveled at how natural it felt. Just three months ago, he'd had such rigid ideas about the perfect wife—someone tall and graceful, from the right family, who knew all the social graces and would make an excellent hostess.

He'd never imagined falling in love with a petite bookseller who walked with a limp and knew more about first editions than about dinner parties.

Yet here was Ivy, whose smile lit up his entire world. She wasn't perfect by society's standards—but who really was? No, Ivy King was perfect for him in all the ways that truly mattered.

Thank You For Reading Perfect!

I hope you enjoyed Will and Ivy's love story. It would mean so much if you would take a quick minute to leave a review! It doesn't have to be long. Just a sentence or two telling what you liked about the story.

To receive a free book and get updates on new releases, go to KimberlyKeagan.com or scan the QR code below and subscribe to my newsletter *The Puddings & Pages Post*.

Acknowledgments

I am thankful for the many blessings in my life, but most of all for my husband, son, and daughter, who love and support me, make me laugh, and keep me grounded.

Thanks, Bob, for being my forever hero. I'm in awe of how forty-one years of marriage have flown by.

A big hug to Kelsy, who created the lovely cover of this debut book and shared her insight so many times along the journey. It's not easy telling your mother what's wrong with her writing!

I'm also grateful for my critique partners, Denise M. Colby, Christina Rich, and Marie Wells Coutu. Your friendship means more to me than I can adequately put into words.

To my incredible launch team friends Tracy Del Campo, Nicole Dunlap, Sophie Leigh Fox, Stephanie Krill, Patricia Long, Alena Mentink, Linda Stevens, Lynne U. Watson, as well as Christina, Denise, and Marie: thank you for cheering me on, offering honest feedback, and walking beside me on this journey. Through prayer, encouragement, and practical help, you got me over the finish line.

A special shout-out to editors Lynne Pearson and Sarah Smith —you are amazing.

Last, but certainly not least, I thank my Lord and Savior, Jesus Christ. To Him be the glory!

About the Author

Kimberly Keagan's love of romance novels started at the age of thirteen. Whenever she could get away with it, she ignored her chores in favor of a story she couldn't put down.

By God's grace, she married her own handsome hero, and together they raised two wonderful children. She earned a degree in accounting and enjoyed a career in investor relations, writing financial reports and press releases. Terrific jobs, but not very romantic.

Now, she's following her dream of writing her own historical romance stories with strong heroines, swoon-worthy heroes, and quirky secondary characters.

When not reading or writing, Kimberly likes to bake, garden, watch sports, and research her family tree.

Also by Kimberly Keagan

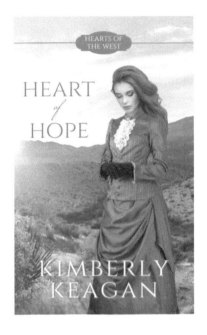

A Philadelphia socialite. A second chance with the man who broke her heart. And a town called Victory that just might live up to its name.

Coming June 10, 2025